MISTRESS

The gown was unusual to say the least. It had been individually designed to Sophie's specifications and radiated dominance, aggressive sensuality, sensual power . . .

The top was of black leather, cut low in the neck and laced tightly at the front. The boning was so subtle it was invisible, yet powerful enough to cinch her waist to eighteen inches and push her breasts upward and outward in bold invitation.

The skirt was full but slashed to the waist, so that if she turned suddenly it opened like the petals of some unholy flower, revealing black-stockinged legs and scarlet spike-heeled boots, laced to the calf.

Sophie picked up the whip. Oh, but it felt good to play the dominatrix!

Mistress

Dagmar Brand

HEADLINE
DELTA

First published in 1996
by HEADLINE BOOK PUBLISHING

A HEADLINE DELTA paperback

10 9 8 7 6 5 4 3 2 1

ISBN 0 7472 4828 1

Typeset at The Spartan Press Ltd,
Lymington, Hants

Printed and bound in Great Britain by
Cox & Wyman Ltd, Reading, Berks

HEADLINE BOOK PUBLISHING
A division of Hodder Headline PLC
338 Euston Road
London NW1 3BH

Mistress

Prologue

Sunlight flooded in as Sophie Ceretto flung open the bedroom windows and leaned out, breathing in the warm, scented air.

'Isn't it wonderful?'

Her lover stepped up behind her, sliding his arms playfully about her waist.

'Not nearly as wonderful as you,' he murmured, and he pressed his lips into the perfect curve of her neck, teasing the silky blonde hairs with the tip of his tongue.

Sophie giggled as his hands moved down over the swell of her buttocks, tense and firm inside white denim jeans.

'Andre . . . Andre, don't!'

'Why not?'

'Because . . .' She laughed, unable to think of any sensible reason why they shouldn't do exactly as they pleased. 'Because we're supposed to be choosing a room for your office, getting things sorted out . . .'

He kissed the nape of her neck again, and felt her shiver with pleasure, pushing her body back against his, softly sliding over and over the swelling tip of his excited manhood. He growled.

1

'I'd rather sort you out, you gorgeous prick-tease.'

This time she gently disengaged from him, turned to face him and pressed her breasts into the hard muscle of his chest.

'You're insatiable, Doctor Grafton. Has anybody ever told you that?'

He caught her hand and pressed her fingers against his lips, licking their very tips as though they were drenched in melting ice cream.

'No. But then again, I'm only insatiable with you.'

He made to grab her and throw her down on to the bed, but she escaped him, twisting her lithe body out of his grasp and running off along the landing to the top of the stairs. He chased her, making sure not to run too fast, because when all was said and done this was a game: a glorious, delicious, self-indulgent game of kiss-chase which he wanted never to end.

This time last year, thought Sophie, she would never have believed that things could be so right for her and Andre Grafton. The strength of her attraction to the brilliant young psychiatrist seemed as nothing compared to the strength of those who had wanted to destroy them.

A few short months ago, her insanely possessive husband Paolo had been threatening vengeance on them both, whilst her 'employer', the scheming dominatrix Marta Kolbuszewski, had vowed never to release Sophie from her evil spell. Only perseverance, useful allies and amazing good fortune had brought them through.

Now, as she basked with Andre in the golden sunlight of success, Sophie reflected on all that had happened.

Paolo had been discredited and fled abroad with his mistress, running only hours ahead of the Fraud Squad; utterly humiliated, Marta had gone to ground. Sophie neither knew nor cared where either of them might be. Good riddance. Now all she wanted was to taste freedom . . . and the seductive pleasure of being with Andre, whenever and wherever she chose.

They laughed madly as they chased each other through the many rooms of the Hall – the vast and beautiful house which had once been Paolo Ceretto's and which now belonged to Sophie.

Breathless with laughter and excitement, Sophie paused in the Whispering Gallery.

'How about here?' She ran her fingertips over the surface of a painting of three nudes, ingeniously entwined. 'Don't you think it's just perfect?'

'Here, in an art gallery? You want me to turn this place into a surgery for my clients?' He glanced around, not quite sure whether she was joking or not. One entire wall of the gallery was glass, taking advantage of the superb morning light and offering an unrivalled view to the main road on the other side of the park. 'You want me to get them to tell me all about their sexual problems . . . here?'

Sophie pouted mischievously.

'Just think of all the motorists you'd entertain . . . and you always did enjoy making an exhibition of yourself . . .'

She darted away from him, at the very moment when he pounced to grab her, and ran away down the stairs, along

3

the passageway and into the kitchen, sending pots and pans clattering to the ground.

'Here then?'

He laughed. 'In the kitchen?'

'You can have a lot of fun in a kitchen.'

Sophie picked up a rolling pin, and rolled it lasciviously over the curves of her delectable body. Andre ached with lust at the sight of her full breasts, the flesh beneath the tight grey T-shirt squeezed and flattened by the wooden roller, then re-emerging in all its beautiful plumpness, revealing nipples that had become transformed from flat disks to pert cones which seemed to reach out for his kisses.

'Just think of all the props . . . all the things your clients could use to *show* you what's on their minds . . .'

This time he caught her and did not let her go, pushing her hard against the Welsh dresser so that all the cups and plates clinked and jangled.

'You think that's what I get up to with my patients, do you?'

Her blue eyes twinkled as they met his gaze.

'You're telling me you *don't* screw your patients?' she joked, knowing that he never would. Andre was far too professional to mix business and pleasure. 'Come on, Andre,' she teased. 'They're frigid old maids and you're a gorgeous young sex therapist. They must be crying out for you to show them what they're missing . . .'

His hand sought out the curve of her buttock and squeezed it. This was a game they both enjoyed: she pretended to be jealous and he pandered to her vivid,

4

faintly perverse fantasies of client and therapist. It was one of the many games which turned them on, like whipped double cream dripped on to the strawberry sundae of their pleasure.

'Well . . .'

'You do, don't you?' Her lips reached out and pressed themselves against his, her tongue-tip working its way between them and into the hot cavern of his mouth. 'Tell me what you do in that consulting room of yours . . .'

'I'd rather show you.'

A shudder of complete pleasure passed through her body and communicated itself to his. He pressed hard against her, showing her with touch how much he wanted her.

She groaned. It felt so good, *sooo* good. No one else came close. Her fingers stretched out to unzip him, to take him into her hands and possess his pleasure; but he shook his head and caught her hands, grinning.

'I'm the therapist, remember? You have to do what I say.'

With gentle firmness he spun her round and pushed her forward over the kitchen table. She sprawled on her belly on the scrubbed oak, feeling the roughness of the wood grain rubbing her nipples through her thin cotton shirt. *Mmm, it felt incredible.* She waggled her arse and Andre responded by reaching round and unbuttoning her jeans.

He pulled them down over her backside.

'What! No panties? What a hussy you are . . .'

His fingertip felt cold as it traced the deep crease between her buttocks, and she realised that he had dipped it into the cream jug and was daubing her with the thick, cold oiliness. She felt it dripping down between her bum-cheeks, anointing her secret 'O' and trickling slowly down to join the honeyed wetness oozing from her sex.

A whispered zizz announced that Andre had unzipped his pants. Sophie's heart thumped with anticipation. And then the anticipation turned to delight as the hot tip of Andre's manhood pushed its way between her thighs, scything into the welcoming haven of her sex.

Yes, yes, yes! she cried out silently in the paradise of her pleasure. And she wondered how much better life could get.

Chapter 1

The steam room at the Club Lazarus was an exclusive haven where tired executives could relax and forget their cares for an hour or two. But its formula did not promise universal success. Amid the swirling clouds of white vapour, two men were deep in edgy conversation.

'The current situation is intolerable,' snapped the middle-aged man.

'It will be resolved,' his younger companion assured him.

'It had better be.'

'You don't trust my judgement?'

The older man paused.

'For the moment, at least, it seems I have little choice.'

His companion rolled over on to his belly on the slatted bench, reached out for a bundle of birch twigs and began lashing them hard against his skin. They brought the blood rushing to the surface, leaving it tingling and buzzing with vibrant life.

'You worry too much,' he suggested, pausing in his endeavours to savour the zing of pleasure as the hot steam caressed his invigorated flesh. 'Just leave everything to me.' Snapping his fingers, he summoned a girl from the shadows.

The girl moved soundlessly towards him, her head demurely bowed. He surveyed her with a critic's eye, appraising her perfect oriental figure, the glossy shoulder-length hair wet with steam and heavy with trickles of warm water which ran down over her arms and dripped from the crests of her pert little breasts. She wore nothing but a pair of black tanga briefs, an ankle chain and white stilettos. *What a little tart*, he thought to himself as he beckoned her to his side. *What a perfect little whore.*

'This is the latest one?'

The older man nodded.

'Fresh in from Bangkok. Very . . . compliant.'

'Nice. Very nice. You have excellent taste.' He beckoned the girl closer. 'You can give me a massage now.'

'Yes sir.'

'And make it a good one.'

She lifted dark, slanted eyes to his. They gave nothing away. She seemed distant, dazed.

'Of course, sir. I am trained to give you pleasure.'

He lay back and let her slip the towel from round his waist, confident that she would be suitably impressed by the dimensions of his manhood. He was eagerly erect for her, the fat purple dome of his prick slick with wetness.

The girl took up a bar of soap and lathered it, working the creamy bubbles over her palms and between her fingers; tantalising him into an agony of expectation before she even laid a hand on him. When she finally

touched him, curling her soapy fingers about the thickness
of his shaft, he damn near shouted out with pleasure. She
was good, even he had to admit that. Damned good.

The older man raised himself to a sitting position on his
bench, the better to watch the spectacle. He loved to
watch; it really turned him on. Untying his towel, he
bared his crotch and began to play with himself. He'd
bring himself off a couple of times and then he'd be ready
for the bitch. Ready to give her a seeing-to she wouldn't
forget in a hurry.

'Something has to be done,' he said. 'And soon.'

His companion shrugged. Frankly he had other things
on his mind right now, like the incredible build-up of
pleasure in his dick, and the red-painted pout of the
oriental girl's lips as she stooped to go down on him.

'It will be, I told you.'

'Talk's cheap. Sophie and Grafton have to pay for what
they've done.' His voice darkened. 'Sophie, especially.'

'Yeah, yeah, OK. Consider it done.'

'Get them out. Get them out of the Hall, destroy them,
make them pay. Understand? I'm a patient man, but my
patience won't last for ever.'

He nodded, but in reality his mind was somewhere a
long way away, falling through space in a multicoloured
burst of shooting stars as his dick twitched and exploded
into the girl's practised mouth.

'Sure. Sure.'

His companion turned away, his face contorted in jealous anger. Reaching out for the tongs, he used them to
pick up a hissing, red-hot coal. Looking down through the

steam, he observed a naked girl sprawling bound and gagged on the floor at his feet. Her eyes widened in fear as she saw him lift the coal, watching it glowing red in the metal jaws of the tongs.

'You understand don't you, my pretty one?'

The girl nodded vigorously, never taking her eyes from the glowing coal.

'Good. I knew you would.'

And opening the jaws of the tongs, he dropped the hot coal into her squirming lap.

Sophie glanced into the mirror and patted her hair as she passed. She looked good – at least, she hoped she did. She had taken a long time getting ready this morning. Today was a big day for Andre and she didn't intend letting him down.

Andre's sex-therapy practice was taking time to establish, but slowly it was getting off the ground. When they'd received a call from Professor Hal Treves, they both knew that things were beginning to go their way. With clients of the Professor's calibre, word would soon get round that Andre Grafton was *the* therapist in town.

The periwinkle-blue suit was cut close to her admirable curves, and the silk blouse felt slinky and sexy next to her bare skin. She wasn't wearing a bra because she loved the feel of raw silk rubbing across her nipples. Lace-topped stockings and strappy shoes completed the outfit, and she had rolled her long blonde hair into a French pleat, leaving just a couple of wavy strands free to fall over her shoulders, softening the look.

'What do you think?' she asked Andre as he came rushing down the passageway, still knotting his tie.

He stopped in his tracks, his face breaking into a lopsided grin.

'Fantastic.' He drew her to him and slid a hand about her waist. 'Do I get to take you to bed right now?'

'Careful!' she laughed. 'You'll smudge my make-up.'

'I'll do more than that if you let me.' His hand groped her backside, apple-firm and tantalising beneath her short skirt. 'Hey, are you wearing any knickers?'

'Should I be?' she enquired innocently.

He groaned in mock agony as he slid up her skirt and let his hand explore the bounty underneath.

'Stockings and lacy suspenders . . . and no panties! Sophie Ceretto, you could drive a man crazy.'

'As long as I drive *you* crazy, darling . . .'

'Oh you do, you do. Come upstairs with me right now and I'll show you how crazy.'

She returned his kiss but drew away, every bit as frustrated as Andre was not to be able to take this any further. She ached for him, her nipples tingling for the caress of his tongue . . . but some things had to wait.

'Later,' she promised him.

'Now,' he protested, slipping his finger between her buttocks and tickling her with mischievous lust.

'Andre,' she pleaded through her giggles. 'We can't, not this minute, there really isn't time . . .'

As though to confirm that what she said was true, her words were cut short by the sound of the doorbell.

'That'll be him.' She kissed Andre, adjusted his tie and

turned to walk to the door. 'I'll let him in. You get things ready in the consulting room.'

She hesitated for a few seconds before opening the front door. The dark line of a man's silhouette was clearly visible through the stained glass panels. Tall, dark, sophisticated – that was how Professor Treves was seen by women all over the country. The sexy face of academia, that was Hal Treves: the thinking woman's pin-up; the hunky lecturer and TV presenter solely responsible for the booming trade in archaeology books. Would he be as desirable as he seemed on the television screen?

Opening the door, Sophie saw that he was. His smile was warm and sexy, his blue-grey eyes sparkling as he extended a hand.

'Good morning – Hal Treves. I've come to see ... er ... Doctor Grafton?'

He seemed edgy to Sophie, but then that was to be expected. *Not half as edgy as I feel though*, she told herself, squeezing her thighs together so that the lobes of her sex closed and rubbed, titillating the head of her clitoris. *Edgy and horny*.

'Yes of course, Professor. Won't you come in? I'll just take your coat.'

'Doctor Grafton is, you know, entirely ... discreet? I have your assurance of that?'

'Complete confidentiality is assured. Doctor Grafton has the highest professional standards.' Even as she reassured him, Sophie was wondering what peculiar sexual peccadillo had driven a man like Hal Treves to seek help. What sexual problems could a man like him possibly have? He was sex on legs.

'Do come this way. Doctor Grafton is waiting for you in his consulting room.'

Ushering him inside, Sophie turned to leave. But the itch of curiosity had been roused – and, besides, what woman in her right mind would miss an opportunity to listen to Hal Treves baring his soul in that soft, seductive voice? She knew from experience that if she just *happened* to go into the filing room to collect a client's records, she'd be bound to hear every word through the thin partition wall.

Andre got to his feet and shook hands with Hal Treves.

'Mr Treves, a pleasure to meet you. Please . . . take a seat, make yourself comfortable.'

'Thank you.' Treves shifted uneasily in his seat. At this moment comfort was not uppermost in his mind. 'You're perhaps wondering why a man like myself . . .'

Andre shook his head.

'It isn't my job to wonder, Professor. Only to listen and offer whatever help I can. So please, don't feel uncomfortable about opening up to me. We all have problems and we all feel awkward about revealing them. You just have to get used to the idea that you can trust me. Now, where shall we start?'

Treves looked up.

'I have . . . urges.' He swallowed and loosened his collar. 'Unusual urges.'

Andre folded his hands.

'Please. Take as much time as you need.'

Treves passed his hand over his forehead.

'I . . . this is very difficult.'

'Yes. Of course.' Andre got up, walked across to the drinks cabinet and poured two measures of brandy. 'Will you join me? It's a rather good Armagnac.'

'Thanks.' Treves took the glass gratefully, and downed half of the brandy in a single gulp. He let out his breath in a long sigh. 'This is going to sound ludicrous to you.'

'I doubt it.'

'It's . . . my students.'

'You have sexual feelings towards them?'

Treves nodded.

'Young women?'

This time Treves paled slightly.

'Yes. Not any one of them in particular, you understand . . . all of them. Pretty ones, ugly ones, flat-chested ones, busty ones – it doesn't seem to matter.'

'You want to have sex with them?'

'N-no. Not exactly. Well . . .'

Andre waited. He knew from experience that if he put pressure on Treves, he would probably clam up completely and never reveal what was bothering him. He tried another tack.

'You find these young woman attractive?'

'Yes.'

'What exactly is it about them that you're attracted to?'

The Professor hesitated for what seemed like an hour, but couldn't have been more than ten seconds.

'Their . . .' He swallowed. 'Their beautiful backsides. The way they . . . quiver when they walk. The way they

14

move inside those tight pants they wear.'

'You want to touch their backsides?' Andre noticed that Treves was sweating slightly, and his hand was trembling as he laid it on the table. 'Their bare backsides?'

'I want to . . . oh God, Doctor, this sounds ridiculous. I want to . . . *spank* them. Can you believe that? I have this terrible urge to take them one by one and put them across my knee . . .'

'Go on.'

'And throw up their skirts and pull down their little panties and then . . . and then thrash them until they're scarlet all over . . .' He groaned. 'I'm a sick pervert, aren't I?'

Andre smiled slightly.

'I wouldn't say that.' *And neither would you, if you'd heard some of the things I've heard*, he added in the silence of his thoughts. 'And what else?'

'Isn't that enough?'

'Tell me what else you want to do, Hal. I think you have other urges, don't you?'

'W-when I've done with spanking them, I want to . . . you know . . . I want to screw them from behind.'

'I see.' Andre leaned forward. He hoped Hal Treves couldn't tell that he, too, was beginning to be excited by Hal's obsession. But then again, what red-blooded male could resist the image of a luscious nineteen-year-old girl lying across his lap with her panties round her ankles and her bare buttocks in the air? 'So tell me – have you actually put any of these fantasies into practice?'

At this, Hal's expression turned to horror.

'Are you crazy, Doctor? Have you any idea what that kind of thing could do to my career?'

'You've never spanked a girl?'

'No. No, never. Well, only a prostitute or two, when things have got really bad, but it's not the same. It's the students I want, nobody else will do. Sometimes the urge is so strong I can hardly stand it, but I've never dared make a move. Hell, Doctor, you have to understand, I have a reputation to protect. And my media career is really starting to take off. There's even talk of a series for American TV ... what am I going to do if all this gets out?'

His voice rose to a hysterical gasp and he had to take a gulp of brandy to steady his nerves.

'OK, Hal, everything's OK.' Andre got to his feet and walked across to the window. 'Everything's going to be just fine.'

'You really think you can help me?'

'Of course I can, that's my job. Now, why don't you lie down on the couch and we'll begin with a little relaxation, then we'll continue with a hypnotherapy session.'

An hour later, as Hal Treves's BMW was disappearing down the driveway towards the main road, Sophie came back into Andre's office. She winked.

'So the darling Mr Treves has a secret urge to spank girls' bottoms! Who'd have thought it?'

She came in and perched on the edge of Andre's desk. He pulled her forward and planted a huge kiss on her lips.

'You've been listening, you bad girl.'

'You know you like me bad. And I'm very, *very* discreet.'

Andre stroked her bottom playfully.

'How did I do?'

'Brilliantly. But you did surprise me.'

'Surprised you? How?'

'Telling Hal Treves you could cure him of his urges.'

'Well, I can – or at least I can help him to control them so he doesn't get himself into deep shit.'

'I think you should just tell him to get on with it and have a really good time!' Sophie declared mischievously.

Andre unfastened the top button of her blouse and darted little kisses into the shadowed valley between her bobbing breasts.

'You minx! You know darned well, if a man like Hal Treves goes round spanking teenage girls and the *Sunday Comet* gets hold of the story, he's finished!'

'Then what he needs is an understanding girlfriend,' Sophie declared.

'What – oh, you mean a girl who *likes* being spanked?'

'Of course!' She laughed at the expression on Andre's face. 'Come on, Andre, you're supposed to be the sex expert, not me. Believe me, there are *lots* of girls who'd just love to have their bottoms spanked by the gorgeous Hal Treves...' She licked her lips lasciviously. 'In the line of duty, of course.'

'Oh, of course! And I suppose you'd be just the girl for the job?'

Sophie slid off the desk, revealing an inch or two of bare

thigh as the hem of her skirt slipped above the lacy top of her stocking.

'Spanking can be fun,' she purred. 'We've never actually tried it, have we?'

'Can't recall that we have.'

Leaning forward over the desk, Sophie pushed out her adorable backside. The blue skirt was stretched tightly across the firm, womanly globes, and Andre could clearly make out the deep, inviting cleft between them.

She turned her head and looked back at him, over her shoulder.

'Then maybe we should.'

She wiggled her backside and Andre's cock wiggled in sympathy. Oh, but she was irresistible: a potent combination of vulnerability, mischief and deep eroticism. With one flick of her tongue, one pout of her lips, one sway of her hips, she could enslave him for ever. She could squat on his face and stifle him with those creamy buttocks, and he'd die a happy man.

Hungrily he pushed up her skirt, revealing the perfect beauty of her arse-cheeks. They were provocatively bare, their plump flawlessness framed by the white lace of her suspender belt and the ornate tops of her stockings. The skin was the colour of clotted cream, and very smooth. He ran the flat of his hand over it, and watched it become goosepimpled as the tiny hairs erected themselves at the lightness of his touch.

'You're a witch, Sophie Ceretto. You must be.'

'If I'm a witch you'll have to punish me for my wickedness, won't you?'

Her blue eyes twinkled and she ran the tip of her tongue over her lips. Somewhere at the back of her mind, a voice whispered darkly of the days when Marta Kolbuszewski's hand had dealt the punishment; when Sophie had railed against it and sworn never to submit to anyone ever again . . . but the habit of chastisement is a hard one to break, and the bad memories swiftly faded to a warm, seducing glow.

'Sophie, I . . .'

'Go on, Andre – punish me. Smack me on my bare bottom, you know I've been a bad, bad girl.'

Raising his hand, he brought it down hesitantly on Sophie's rump. The effect he found astonishing. It bewitched him utterly to see her backside leap up, her buttocks quivering as the skin marbled pink and white; to smell the sweet odour of her excitement as her thighs slid a little further apart, revealing the glistening wetness of her sex. His cock ached and, as he struck her again, more confidently this time, it pushed its swollen head against the inside of his pants, rubbing itself rather painfully against the ridged inner surface of his zipper.

Thwack. Thwack. Slap. Smack. His hand fell again and again, faster and faster, harder and harder; and he discovered that if he cupped his hand slightly, he could strike her with much greater effect, making her gasp and moan with the delicious discomfort.

'Bad. Bad. *Bad* girl,' he gasped, and she pushed her backside out even further, in an invitation he simply couldn't refuse.

Unzipping his pants, he took out his manhood, cradling

it in the palm of his hand. It felt hot and urgent, throbbing with a pulsing ache which demanded to be satisfied.

'Want me?' he whispered.

'Want you. Now.' She rubbed her backside against the tip of his cock, smearing the taut, reddened flesh with his glistening moisture. Her backside felt red-hot even against the throbbing heat of his erection; he felt feverish, hungry, insatiable.

With a soft groan of satisfaction, he slid into her up to the hilt. Pushing herself back on to the shaft of his cock, Sophie looked round at him and smiled.

'You see, Andre? I told you spanking could be fun.'

Over the next few weeks, Andre and Sophie really worked at the business, and began to make a go of it. As income picked up, they were even able to employ a receptionist: a bubbly brunette called Stephanie Lace.

OK, so clients weren't exactly flooding to Andre's exclusive clinic, or at least not yet, but he was slowly building up an appreciative clientele. The only thing they really lacked, to make the whole enterprise take off, was a big-name client who was prepared to go public: someone whose patronage would attract others to the clinic.

Someone like Lady Anastasia Madeley.

Andre was alone in his consulting room one day when Stephanie burst in.

'Doctor Grafton!'

He looked up.

'Stephanie – how many times have I told you to knock

before you come in? I could be in the middle of a consultation!'

'Sorry, Doctor Grafton, only . . . there's someone to see you.'

He glanced at the diary.

'I don't have any appointments until twelve. There must be some mistake.'

'No mistake, Doctor. She says she's come specially and she won't leave until she's seen you!'

'She?'

'Lady Madeley, Doctor. Lady Anastasia Madeley!'

Anastasia Madeley? Andre's heart thumped as he got to his feet, straightening his tie. *The* Lady Anastasia, adventuress, erotic novelist, legendary partygoer, media darling . . .? If it really was her, and he could persuade her to become one of his clients . . .

Dismissing Stephanie, he hurried into the waiting room, only to stop dead in his tracks.

There was only one person in the waiting room, but her presence seemed to fill it. Lady Anastasia Madeley was five feet ten inches of pure, auburn-haired sex, and she was curled up on *his* leather chesterfield; her long legs tucked up underneath her, revealing an expanse of thoroughbred thigh.

'Doctor Grafton, how lovely of you to see me.' She got to her feet, stretching herself out like a cat, lazily muscular and sensually aware.

At the sight of her, his jaw almost hit the floor. She was at least ten times more sultry and more gorgeous than in any of her photographs or television appearances. Not to

mention utterly screwable. He felt like a hormone-
charged adolescent as he ushered her into his consulting
room and shut the door.

'Please, Lady Anastasia – do take a seat.'

'How kind.'

She arranged herself in one of his antique chairs, to
such good effect that he found himself obliged to look
down the front of her low-cut green velvet suit.

'How can I help you?'

At this, Lady Anastasia's expression became serious,
her tone of voice an almost desperate whisper.

'Oh Doctor . . . Doctor, I just don't know who I can
turn to.'

Mesmerised by Lady Anastasia's green eyes and moist,
scarlet lips, Andre drew up a chair, sitting down beside
her.

'Something is wrong? Something . . . sexual?'

He could hardly believe what he was saying. Wasn't
Lady Anastasia Madeley known as a sex-siren, the fulfil-
ment of every man's ultimate fantasy?

She nodded.

'As you know, Doctor Grafton, I am known as a
woman of passion, of . . .' She paused. 'A certain . . .
reputation.'

Andre's mouth was dry. Was it him, or was it really
getting hot in his consulting room? He eased the collar
away from his constricted throat with a shaking finger.

'I'm sorry, Lady Anastasia. I don't quite understand.'

'Neither do I, Doctor, and there lies my problem. You
see, I seem to have lost my . . . enthusiasm.' She reached

out a hand whose nails were dangerously scarlet, and laid it upon his knee. 'And I was rather hoping you might be the man to find it for me. In fact—' She smiled. 'I *know* you are.'

Chapter 2

Trixie hadn't been expecting anything quite like this.

Being gagged – that was all right, she'd done that with loads of the punters from the Pink Pearl Club and you got used to it. Being tied up? Well, that could be quite a lot of fun with the right guy . . . and Trixie knew a lot of guys.

But being bound, gagged, blindfolded and thrown forwards over a pool table, now *that* was something which took a lot of getting used to – especially when your nipples were squashed into the baize and your naked quim was rubbing up against one of the pockets.

As a matter of fact, it was kind of sexy. Quite unexpectedly, Trixie heard a woman's voice giggle. She giggled even more when she realised it was her own voice. Obviously they'd slipped her something in that pink champagne and it had taken away what few inhibitions she'd ever had, making her body tingle all over and filling her fluffy head with the most incredible fantasies. She felt so silly . . . and so sexy. So horny she'd have fucked any man who asked her, not that she had to, because they weren't giving her much opportunity to have her say. Strange, unseen hands were pawing her, gruff voices discussed her, but they all seemed so far away.

'She's good. Very nice arse.'

'And those tits – like Zeppelins. Natural, are they?'

'Home-grown, I swear on my mother's life. No en-hancements, feel them for yourself.'

'And she's only seventeen, you say?'

'She's a big girl for her age. And she sucks cock like an angel.'

'Yeah, but can she take it up the arse? My clients like them versatile.'

'Believe me, she likes nothing better. She's a dirty-minded little bitch, her brains are all in her snatch.'

Trixie giggled into the silk scarf which had been tied across her mouth. It all seemed silly, some sort of mad game, something in a dream which would go away when she woke up. She made up her mind to enjoy it now, while she had the chance.

Oh, how her quim was aching. She wanted to rub it harder and harder to ease the agony of frustration. Better still, she wanted a nice big dick to fill her up and make her come. As much from instinct as conscious thought, Trixie began tilting her hips, rubbing her wet labia against the iron hoop of the pool pocket.

A man's voice chuckled.

'Hot little bitch! Look, she's trying to bring herself off.'

'That's enough of that!' Something struck Trixie's back-side a stinging blow, and she leapt up with a startled cry, more titillated than chastised. 'You'll have to learn better discipline, my girl.'

That voice . . . Somewhere in the muddied swirl of

Trixie's thoughts, she was sure she recognised that man's voice. Wasn't it . . .? Wasn't it that bloke who used to hang around the Pink Pearl when Sophie worked there? The one who . . .? What was his name . . .?

What the hell, she thought lazily as the hands roamed over her nakedness. What did it matter who he was? His fingernails felt so nice on her skin, clawing stinging furrows down her back and buttocks. She growled her pleasure as strong hands forced her head down, pushing her face into the baize. Her clitoris was throbbing, begging for release; and when a huge, hard prick forced its way between her buttocks and sought out the secret heart of her pleasure, she could have screamed with delight.

She floated in a limbo of dreamy eroticism. Oh how lovely it felt to be held down and buggered. How ever did they guess that this was exactly what she'd always wanted? Who gave a toss what was going on, or who these men were?

The sex was just about perfect.

Sophie stretched out in the bed, rolled on to her side and blinked sleepily at the clock. 3.17. It was dark, warm, comfortable – so why couldn't she sleep? She flicked on the bedside lamp, casting a rosy glow over the brass bedstead, the soft white carpet, the exquisite collection of Lalique glassware on the dressing table.

As she drifted closer to wakefulness, she became aware of Andre, talking fitfully to himself as he tossed and turned in his sleep. What was that he was saying?

'Can't . . . no more. Can't . . .'

Alarmed now, Sophie grabbed him by the shoulders and shook him into consciousness.

'Andre! Andre, what's wrong?'

He jolted awake, gazing at her for a few seconds unseeing, not recognising anything around him. She saw that there were beads of sweat on his brow.

'I . . .'

'Andre. You were having a bad dream.'

His tense body seemed to deflate, and he sank back on to the pillows.

'Go back to sleep, it was nothing, honestly.'

'No. There's more to it than that. You haven't had a decent night's sleep in over a week.'

Refusing to be palmed off with feeble excuses, Sophie slipped down into the bed beside him, pulling the satin sheet over them as she slid her body against his until she lay on her side, her belly against his flank. Slowly she raised her leg, curling her thigh across his hips. Her fingers stroked the side of his face.

'Come on, Andre. I thought we said we'd never have secrets between us.'

He took her hand and kissed it.

'I just don't want you worrying, that's all.'

'Worrying? About what? Look, Andre, if there's something worth worrying about, I want to know what it is.' She softened her tone, slinkily caressing his belly with her thigh, rubbing herself up against him, coaxing out the truth.

He rolled over so that he too was on his side, facing her, their bodies locked by Sophie's thigh, hooked around his hips, and his embracing arm. He let his hand slide down her bare back, reminding himself of the incredible thrill of just touching her; of how amazingly lucky he was to have what he had. And yet . . .

'It's probably nothing,' he began, stroking the nape of her neck and letting his hand fall gently down from neck to waist and backside.

'If it's nothing, why keep it from me?'

'All right,' he surrendered. 'It's the practice. There are . . . problems. Money problems.'

'All businesses have financial problems when they start up.' Sophie pushed her belly against Andre's, delighting in the firmness of muscle beneath his smooth, tanned skin.

'It's more than that,' insisted Andre. 'We're slipping into debt. If things go on like this . . .'

'They won't.' She stopped his mouth with a kiss. 'You're beginning to attract some really wealthy and influential clients. There's Hal Treves . . . and Lady Anastasia . . .'

'Two clients aren't enough to keep this place going.' His gaze moved around the room, taking in the ornate beauty of the place. The *expensively* ornate beauty. 'Sophie, we may have the Hall, but that's all we have – no capital, nothing else. I'm flying by the seat of my pants, and that makes me incredibly nervous.'

'You shouldn't be.'

'Oh yes I should. What if I let you down?'

She smiled, her blue eyes luminous in the rose-pink glow from the lamp.

'You won't. I trust you completely.'

'Yes, but . . .'

'But nothing. Everything will be fine.' *And if it isn't I shall make it fine*, she thought to herself. *There's no way that Paolo Ceretto is ever going to enjoy another victory over us.*

She turned her attentions to Andre.

'You're cold. Come closer, I want to get you all warm again.'

Taking him into her arms, she cradled his head, covering his face with kisses. He let out a low moan as she took his head between her ample breasts, caressing and enfolding it, stroking it as she rubbed her body against his.

'Everything's fine,' she repeated. And sliding down his body and underneath the sheet, she rolled him on to his back with firm and gentle insistence. 'Now I'm going to make you feel really, really good. Just relax and let me do everything.'

Only a faint pink glow filtered through the white satin sheet, but the outline of his manhood showed up distinctly against the darkness of his wiry pubic curls. Andre Grafton's penis was beautiful even in repose: not enormously sized, but certainly larger than average, its beauty resided above all in its shape. It was long and thick, offering the promise of a delicious fucking; yet so far it had hardly responded to her caresses.

She knelt over him, pushing apart his thighs so that she could kneel between them. Her hands traced the firm, muscular curves of belly, hip and thigh; her fingers teasing tanned flesh.

'Don't you want me, Andre?' she breathed.

He groaned, his body alternately tensing and relaxing as her hands smoothed over it, rediscovering curves and plains and hollows that they knew so well.

'Sophie . . . Sophie, you *witch*! How do you do this to me?'

She laughed and, stooping, began to lick his belly.

'Don't ask questions, Andre. Just lie back and enjoy it.'

At first she flicked her tongue-tip with the lightest of strokes across his bare flesh, erecting the dark, curly hairs which led from his navel to the thick tangle of pubic hair. He writhed in pleasure under her spell now, his penis beginning to respond to her seduction; stiffening and uncurling like a waking serpent.

His balls seemed to offer themselves to her hands. They were large, almost equal in size and very heavy within their tense purse of flesh, deliciously enclosed by dark and curling hairs. She squeezed and fondled them, rolling them about in her hands, gently rubbing them with the flat of her thumb, feeling the trembling intensity of Andre's desire, rippling through him and into her.

She felt his excitement communicate itself to her. Her breasts hung low over Andre's belly as she licked him, their fullness distended from roundness to a heavy pear-shape. Each breast was tipped by a stalk of swollen and hardened flesh which lightly grazed Andre's belly as it swung from side to side.

Bending a little lower, she took Andre's penis in her hand and began stroking it. It responded with a sudden eagerness, the last softness disappearing as the flesh swelled into instant rigidity. She rubbed her thumb over the glans and found it wet and weeping, its slippery fluid abundant and eager. She smeared it over his cock-tip and shaft, and began masturbating him with a tantalising gentleness of touch.

'Harder . . . oh, Sophie, don't do this to me! You have to do it harder, you're driving me insane!'

'But you love me to drive you insane, Andre. You know you do.'

And it was true. As he writhed on the bed under Sophie's unrelenting caresses, Andre's mind began to empty of the tormenting anxieties which had disturbed his nights and days for several weeks. Perhaps Sophie was right, and there really was nothing to worry about. Perhaps everything would turn out fine, the entire Royal Family would sign up for a course of psychotherapy, and their fortunes would be made. It was hard to see the world in shades of black when your beautiful, sexy, irresistible lover was bending over you, opening her glossy mouth to capture the tip of your eager penis . . .

Sophie formed her lips into a wide 'O' of welcome, and bent to take Andre's manhood into her mouth. She began by taking only the very tip between her lips, holding it fast whilst her tongue flicked over and around it, teasing, caressing, coaxing, holding out the promise of blissful release and yet never taking her lover quite close enough for him to reach out and grab it.

She knew all the skills of lovemaking. She had had excellent teachers – but that was in the past. Marta and Laszlo, Paolo and Rick and the Pink Pearl, they were part of a bad dream and, like Andre, she had awoken from her nightmare and was never going to give in to it, ever again.

With a swift, scything movement, she went down on Andre, pushing her face down on him so that his cock shot upwards and back into her throat, filling her up. His saltiness tasted good and she sucked hard, filling herself with the taste and the scent and the feel of him.

The fingers of her left hand cupped his balls, whilst with her right index finger she traced the deep and tempting furrow which ran from balls to arse. How Andre twisted and turned as she ran her fingernail between his buttocks, drawing it forward again and again.

He began thrusting, lifting his backside off the bed as his hips bucked, pushing his cock-tip further into her, until it was nudging against the back of her throat. She welcomed him in, wishing that she could take him even deeper inside her; and in her mind she saw herself taking a giant dick into her mouth, her throat, her belly, so that it passed right through her body and impaled her, emerging from between her parted thighs. At this thought a flood of juice gushed from her swollen sex and trickled down her thighs to moisten the white satin on which she knelt.

Andre's strong hands gripped her head, pushing her down onto him.

'Don't stop ... don't stop. Oh, Sophie, Sophie, you darling, I'm going to come right down your throat ...'

Curling her fingers about the base of his shaft, she began working it up and down, masturbating him slowly and with control, refusing to let him come until she was good and ready.

'Ah. Aaah. Oh yes, can't you feel it? The spunk's rising in my balls, it feels like it's boiling hot . . .'

Just when he was at the point of explosion, Sophie took his cock from her mouth and squeezed the tip hard between finger and thumb. Andre let out a gasp and tightened his grip on her shoulders.

'Sophie . . . what the hell?'

She laughed.

'Just making it last, darling. I want to make sure you *really* enjoy it when you come.'

He groaned in mock agony; but already Sophie was sucking him again, bringing him tantalisingly close to the point of ejaculation then denying him that final mercy. Three times she brought him to crisis-point, and only when he was almost weeping with frustration did she relent, caressing his balls as she licked and sucked him to a shivering, shuddering climax.

Andre lay flat on his back, eyes closed, breathing heavily. Sophie clawed her way up his body until she was lying on top of him. She kissed him.

'Good, huh?'

His eyes flicked open.

'You're a wicked girl, Sophie Ceretto.'

'Complaining?'

'Oh definitely.'

With a growl of triumph, he rolled over suddenly, imprisoning Sophie beneath him. His strong hands flipped her on to her belly.

'You always did have a fantastic arse, Sophie.'

She responded by thrusting it out, and on impulse he

leaned over her and bit it, sinking his teeth into her buttock as though it were the firm and juicy flesh of a ripe apple.

'Ow! That hurts.' She pouted at him over her shoulder. 'You big rough brute.'

'But you love it really.'

She smiled.

'Oh yeah? Well, you're going to love this even more.'

Getting up onto her hands and knees, she thrust out her backside, doggy-fashion. With her thighs wide apart, her bum-cheeks opened to reveal the glistening furrow between. He could scarcely have resisted, even if he hadn't been swollen to the point of agony.

'Go on, tiger,' she breathed. 'Take me. I want you. What are you waiting for?'

What indeed? With a growl of satisfaction he slid into her, revelling in the glorious heat from her dripping sex.

Maybe Sophie was right. Maybe everything really was going to be fine, after all.

It was the following day, after breakfast, when Sophie had the idea.

She was flicking through a glossy magazine while she drank coffee, glancing at all the designer clothes she couldn't possibly afford, and the platinum Rolex she'd love to be able to buy Andre for his birthday. Until the business took off, that sort of luxury was out of the question. But what did they need luxuries for anyway? She reminded herself that she'd had everything money could buy when she'd been Mrs Paolo Ceretto, and where had that got her? The gutter, via Heartbreak Hotel, that's where.

Sophie sipped her coffee reflectively. She didn't much enjoy thinking about the bad times but, then again, perhaps it did her good to remember that things hadn't always been easy. First there had been life with Paolo, life as the pampered plaything of a man who'd scorned and disregarded her until the day she became dangerous to him.

Then there had been life on the street; there hadn't been any luxuries then, she reminded herself. She'd been forced to live in a grimy bedsit and work as a cocktail waitress at the Pink Pearl ... until the day she'd been picked up by predatory Marta Kolbuszewski, and turned into her 'maid', her sexual slave ...

No, she decided, setting down her coffee cup in its saucer. No, she was never going to let herself become that vulnerable ever again. She and Andre were going to make it – and she was going to make sure that they did.

She had ... skills. And contacts. There were people who had once helped her out and might be willing to help her out again. She didn't have to just sit around on her backside, waiting for good things to fall into her lap. What good would it do Andre if she left him to sort everything out himself? And what harm could there possibly be if she decided to help Andre out a little, bring a little extra cash into the household?

Caught somewhere between fear and excitement, she picked up her mobile phone. She hesitated for a few moments before switching it on, then dialled and waited.

A girl's voice answered, sing-song and more childlike than sexy.

'Pink Pearl Club, Dee-Dee speaking, can I help you?'

'Yes', said Sophie, swallowing to get the dryness out of her throat. 'I'd like to speak to Laszlo please, Laszlo Comaneci.' She paused. 'It's about a business proposition.'

Lady Anastasia Madeley was paying one of her thrice-weekly visits to Doctor Andre Grafton.

He watched her, trying hard not to drool, as she stretched out those endless legs and arranged herself in the leather armchair. This afternoon she was wearing a particularly striking outfit consisting of a white stretchy body-suit, no bra and a black PVC miniskirt, and it was impossible not to notice the fullness of her breasts, free and mobile beneath their inadequate covering. Lady Anastasia was definitely not your typical aristocrat, he mused as he fiddled with his fountain pen and pretended that he was in a fit state to take notes.

'How are you today, Lady Anastasia?' he enquired, hoping that she would not notice the slight catch in his voice.

'Please, Doctor, we agreed,' she reproached him. 'You promised that you would call me Anastasia. It is so much more . . . intimate.'

'Very well, *Anastasia*. Perhaps you would like to tell me a little of how you have been feeling since our last session? For instance, have you experienced sexual urges?'

Anastasia let out an extravagant sigh and draped herself elegantly over the arm of the chair – a movement which made her breasts jiggle and Andre's libido rise to an unprofessional level. He crossed his legs in the hope that she wouldn't notice.

'Alas . . . no.'

'You don't feel that this course of therapy is doing you any good? These things take time . . .'

'Ah, Doctor Grafton, I am very happy to come to you, we get on *so* well together, but sadly . . .' Her eyes worked their way downwards and lingered for a few seconds on his crotch before moving upwards to meet his gaze. 'Sadly it rather looks as though things aren't going to work out quite as I had planned. I may even have to think about finding myself another doctor . . .'

There was meaning in that look; a lot of meaning – and Andre Grafton was not a stupid man. He took the hint – the same hint that his own sexual desires had been making to him ever since Lady Anastasia had stepped into his consulting room.

He laid down his notebook and pen.

'I see.' He made an effort to look thoughtful – this was after all a game, and there were rules you had to play it by. 'I wonder . . .'

'Yes, Doctor?' Anastasia's face was a picture of innocent curiosity. 'You have an idea which might help me to recover my . . . enthusiasm?'

'I am wondering . . . if perhaps you are unable to feel pleasure at the moment because you have lost the ability to *give* pleasure. Do you understand what I'm saying?'

'I think perhaps I am beginning to.' A smile played at the corners of Anastasia's mouth. 'But how can I begin to

38

learn how to give this pleasure?'

Andre rose to his feet.

'With help,' he replied softly. 'Professional help.'

'Help me, Doctor. I know you can.'

He took her hands and arranged her so that she was sitting on the very edge of the armchair. Reaching out with hands that trembled almost imperceptibly, he unfastened the buttons at the front of her bodysuit and peeled it down over her shoulders.

Her breasts sprang into his hands as though they had longed to be liberated from their confinement. They felt firm, hot, moist; he could smell her perfume, a sexy, musky warmth that flooded his senses and made him randier than a stag in the rutting season. *Was this madness? Maybe.* What was certain was that it was what he wanted to do and he had to take the chance that it was what she wanted too.

'Oh, Doctor,' she breathed, her eyes never leaving his for a moment. 'Whatever must I do?'

His mouth was dry.

'Unzip my flies.' Her long, scarlet-tipped fingers reached out and did as he instructed. 'Now reach inside and touch my cock. Tell me how it feels.'

'Lovely. It feels . . . like it wants me to kiss it.'

'Now take it out.'

She did so, and he almost cried out at the delicious coolness of those aristocratic fingers on his overheated flesh. His cock was so throbbingly full of spunk that he wondered if they would get any further without him coming all over her.

'And now, Doctor? What now?'

Taking Anastasia's breasts in his hands, he slid his cock into the deep valley between them and closed them tight about it, imprisoning his shaft in hot tit-flesh.

'Now you bring me off,' he told her simply and un-smilingly. 'This is an important clinical test. I want you to see if you can give me pleasure.'

She took charge instantly, squeezing her breasts about Andre's shaft as she tit-wanked him, pushing herself back and forth so that her breasts themselves caressed him, and he had nothing to do but simply stand there and abandon himself to the guilty, delicious pleasure.

Anastasia Madeley's skills were legendary, and Andre had ample opportunity to confirm that they had not been overestimated. She kept him on the edge for longer than he could believe possible, but even she could not hold back the tide for ever.

Betraying his extreme pleasure with only the faintest of groans, Andre spurted his jism all over Lady Anastasia's breasts, face and clothes, spattering her with pearly-white patches of wetness.

For a few moments no one moved or spoke. Andre and Anastasia contemplated each other in enigmatic silence. Then Anastasia put out her long pink tongue and licked a trickle of semen from her chin.

'Well, well, Doctor.' She smiled. 'I do believe I'm feeling better already.'

Chapter 3

The Pink Pearl Club wasn't quite as easy to find as Sophie remembered.

It was situated halfway up the same dingy backstreet, but a new, more tasteful facade had replaced the flashing neon sign and the whole place looked ... well ... more prosperous somehow.

Stepping up to the side door, Sophie rang the bell and waited. It seemed odd to be visiting a place like the Pink Pearl in daylight. She remembered it as a place only to be fully appreciated after dark: a place of striking contrasts, of pink fluffiness and dark shadows, of Trixie and Dee-Dee and Rick ... and Laszlo Comaneci.

Footsteps sounded behind the door, and Sophie heard first a chain rattling, then bolts being drawn back. Evidently Laszlo hadn't let up on security since he'd bought Marta's share of the club.

The door opened a fraction.

'Yes?'

'I'm here to see Rick.'

'Oh yeah. He did say summink. You'd better come in.'

The door opened wider, and Sophie stepped inside. The

girl speaking to her was a contrast in herself. Tall, elegant, brunette, she looked the picture of sophistication until she opened her mouth. But, then again, thought Sophie, if you worked at the Pink Pearl you didn't use your mouth for talking.

She extended her hand.

'Sophie Ceretto.'

The girl pushed a ball of chewing gum into her cheek.

'Chrissie. I'm a hostess here. You wanna see Rick now then?'

Sophie nodded. 'We've a little bit of business and it won't wait.'

She followed Chrissie through the side entrance and along the dingy corridors which led to Rick's office, behind the main dance floor and stage. She wondered if it had changed – whether Laszlo had carried out his plan to get rid of all that pink nylon velvet and the topless girls in pink feather g-strings, sitting on gilded swings.

Chrissie knocked on the door of Rick's office. A familiar voice growled.

'Piss off, I'm busy.'

'It's that woman you're seeing, Rick.'

'What woman?'

'You know, Rick – that Sophie woman.'

Sophie heard a chair scraping across a bare floor, and five seconds later the door was open and Rick was ushering her inside; bowing, scraping, almost rupturing himself in an attempt to be welcoming. How different from the days when she'd been a humble hostess, a thorn in Rick's side because she wouldn't get 'a bit more friendly' with the punters.

'Sophie, Sophie, you're looking incredible! Where have you been hiding yourself?' He pushed a scantily dressed nymphette out of the way, and she scuttled out of the office, clutching a pair of crumpled panties. 'We've missed you . . .'

'I'm glad to hear it.'

'Laszlo often talks about you.'

'Really?' She betrayed nothing, though her heart skipped a beat at the thought of dark, mysterious, compelling Laszlo Comaneci. 'And what does he say?'

'You know how it is, Sophie. Laszlo's always carried a torch for you.' Rick's smile broadened, and his hand sneaked a quick grope of Sophie's backside, sleek and firm in a white crepe minidress. 'We all have.'

Sophie took Rick's hand and firmly removed it from her bottom.

'Don't touch what you can't afford,' she said coolly. 'This isn't a personal call – we have business to sort out.'

'Yes, yes, of course – sorry, Sophie.' Rick undid the collar of his shirt. It was a Paul Smith original, but he still managed to look sleazy in it. 'What's all this about, anyhow?'

Sophie perched on the edge of Rick's desk.

'Didn't Laszlo tell you?'

'Not . . . everything, no. Just that you were interested in some of the girls.'

'That's all you need to know.'

Rick studied Sophie's face and figure. He hadn't lied, she really did look fantastic. Her blonde hair framed a perfectly made-up face, dominated by large blue eyes and a sublimely sexy scarlet pout. Her figure was incredible – slender yet curvaceous, with everything in exactly the right places to drive a man wild with lust. *But there was more to Sophie than that*, he told himself. Something irresistible, and now something that was powerful too. She'd come a long way from the tearful victim who'd stumbled into his office a couple of years ago, begging for a job, any job.

'You've changed,' he commented, running a hand through his designer-tousled brown hair.

Sophie smiled.

'You haven't,' she observed archly.

'No, well, if it ain't broke don't fix it, yeah?' His voice softened. 'You and me could have been good together, Soph. We still could, come to that. The punters used to wet their pants just thinking about you . . .'

She laughed.

'Sorry to disappoint you, Rick, but as I said, this is strictly business. Now, Laszlo said you'd have eight or nine of your best girls ready to show me. I hope I haven't come on a wasted errand.'

'No, no, course not.' For all his cockiness, Rick was no fool; and certainly not a big enough fool to risk upsetting Laszlo Comaneci. 'Come right this way, we've got some real stunners for you to look at.'

She followed Rick out into the club.

'Looks like somebody's been spending a lot of money on the old place,' she commented.

'You know Laszlo, don't do anything if you can't do it properly . . . and business has really picked up since we got La Gioconda over from Italy to star in the floor show. You should see what that girl can do with a python and a glass of water.'

Sophie took a seat in the front row, next to the long runway-style stage which Laszlo had had built. Cleverly, she thought, he had retained just enough of the Pink Pearl's kitsch sleaziness to preserve its sexy charm, whilst spending thousands on taking it upmarket. Lighting effects, dry-ice machines, revolving staging, ornate cages in gilded wrought iron ... he'd created a fuzzy pink nightmare in which you could lose yourself so cosily that you might never want to escape.

Rick, meanwhile, was busy pouring glasses of Chardonnay and giving a running commentary.

'OK, Chrissie, you can start the music now.' From somewhere behind the stage a jungle beat pounded out, and the girls began filing on to the stage. 'Now that one at the front, the redhead, that's Dee-Dee – you remember Dee-Dee don't you? She's had offers to star in a live sex show in Bangkok, but she reckons she's not so keen on shagging fat American tourists ...'

Sophie wasn't really listening. Her eyes were running along the line, mentally putting a tick or a cross or a question mark against each girl. No; yes; maybe; not in a million years.

'Shall I put them through their paces for you?'

'Of course. They may look good, but they're no use to me if they can't perform.'

A snap of Rick's fingers brought a couple of magnificent black male dancers on to the stage. Sophie felt a spreading warmth between her thighs as she watched their muscular bodies move sinuously beneath skintight silver shorts. My, but they were big boys; big in every department . . .

Each girl went through her party piece. Sophie had almost ruled out Dee-Dee as too wholesome and un-imaginative – until she stripped the shorts from one of the dancers and started tonguing his backside.

Now *that* was a pretty fine display of exhibitionism, thought Sophie to herself as another girl, dusky-skinned and petite, knelt in front of the dancer and took one of his huge, shaven testicles into her mouth. That *is exactly the kind of enthusiasm I'm looking for in my girls.*

Rick nudged Sophie's arm.

'That's Indhira, great isn't she? The things they teach them in those Bombay brothels, you just wouldn't believe it . . .'

'Really? I rather think I would,' replied Sophie, sipping the chilled white wine as she enjoyed the spectacle of Dee-Dee pulling apart her lover's glossy black buttocks and pushing her incredibly long tongue into his eager anus. So eager, indeed, that he pushed out his glorious arse, forcing it hard against her face. Dee-Dee responded by fucking him with her tongue, piercing him again and again with its pointed tip, clearly relishing her part in his pleasure as her fingernails scratched and squeezed and clawed at his buttocks.

Meanwhile Indhira – not wishing to be outdone – had succeeded in taking both of her lover's testicles into her capacious mouth, and was evidently caressing them with her tongue whilst holding his cock in her two hands and masturbating it with lascivious slowness. As he leant back, offering himself to his two lovers, his body shook with excitement and the three silver rings jingled in his right nipple.

Sophie crossed her legs at the thigh. This afforded her the opportunity to pleasure herself in stealth, squeezing her legs together so that her labia were forced into a delicious friction. If Rick guessed what she was doing, he gave no sign, and simply went on with his sales pitch.

'Then there's Vicky, she's the tall redhead on the end, with the big bazookas. Crush a man to death with them, she could. In fact, in the show, she brings a bloke off with them.'

Vicky? wondered Sophie, making a supreme effort to concentrate on the show and not on the developing pleasure between her legs. Vicky. Her blue eyes scrutinised the girl. A bit on the tall side, and men didn't always go for redheads ... but those breasts, now they were really something special. And the things she was doing. Hell, but that African girl looked to be in Heaven as she licked whipped cream from those dinner-plate nipples.

An orgasm shuddered through her quite unexpectedly and almost uncontrollably. She very nearly dropped her wineglass as the rush of pleasure overtook her, liberating a flood of sweet elixir which soaked the gusset of her white lace panties.

Rick was at her shoulder.

'You OK, Soph?'

'What?'

'You OK, only you looked a bit... I dunno...
vacant.'

She laughed and uncrossed her thighs. She wondered if
he too could smell the spicy sweet odour rising from her
warm quim.

'Just concentrating, Rick. Making up my mind.'

'And have you? Made up your mind, I mean?'

'As a matter of fact I have. I'll take Dee-Dee, Indhira,
Vicky and Tas. Oh, and Trixie of course.' Sophie gave
Rick a knowing smile. 'I know how you like to keep her to
yourself.'

'Actually...' began Rick. 'Actually, there might be a
problem with Trixie.'

'Problem? What sort of problem?'

'It's a bit awkward, Soph. You see, she's disappeared.
Vanished off the face of the earth.'

Laszlo Comaneci's personal assistant, Davina Templeton,
was not exactly over the moon about her latest assignment.

She was clearly a cut above that blonde chancer Sophie
Ceretto, and being told that she must spend several weeks
helping Sophie to set up her new business venture didn't
go down at all well – particularly since she knew damn
well that Laszlo had never got over his ridiculous infatua-
tion with Sophie. It was too bad, just too damn bad, and
she wasn't going to put up with it a moment longer than
she had to. Laszlo was hers, and she certainly wasn't going
to let Sophie bloody Ceretto get her claws into the poor
besotted idiot.

They were sitting in Sophie's car, outside an empty shop on the wealthy side of town.

'Well, how about this one?' Sophie picked the specification from the sheaf in her lap, and handed it to Davina. 'What do you think?'

Davina sniffed. 'What am I supposed to think?'

'You're *supposed* to be helping me – or shall I tell Laszlo you'd prefer not to?' Sophie enquired sweetly.

'I suppose it might do.' Davina glanced at the sheet of paper. 'It says here that it was once used to make and sell exclusive leatherwear.'

A smile crossed Sophie's face.

'Perfect. It must be an omen. Come on, Davina, let's take a look. We need to find suitable premises soon, so we can actually start making some money.'

Unlocking the front door, they stepped inside. The smell of fine leather filled the place, acrid yet strangely sensual.

'Well?' enquired Sophie, opening doors and peering into storerooms, workrooms, changing rooms. 'What's your verdict?'

Davina sighed.

'I suppose it will do,' she replied. 'If you're quite determined that you want to do . . . this sort of thing. Still, I suppose if it's all you know how to do . . .'

'Some people don't have any choice,' replied Sophie pointedly. 'We don't all have a multi-millionaire property developer keeping us in the lap of luxury.'

'Oh, and precisely what is *that* supposed to mean?'

'Whatever you want it to mean,' replied Sophie sweetly.

At that moment the doorbell jingled and a third figure stepped into the shop; the figure of a man somewhere in his early to mid forties, dark-haired, high-cheekboned, tall and broad-shouldered. At the sight of him, Davina's entire personality was instantly transformed.

'Laszlo!' She arranged her face into a charming smile. 'We weren't expecting you.'

'No, well, I thought I'd come along and keep an eye on my investment.' To Davina's fury, his grey eyes drifted from her to Sophie, lingering far too long before moving on to survey the interior of the shop. 'So – are you going to take this?'

'I think so,' replied Sophie. 'It should suit us very well after a little refurbishment. Why don't you take a look at the floor measurements?'

Laszlo moved a little closer to Sophie. Their hands touched as she handed him the specification. Davina bristled, but Sophie was indifferent and Laszlo seemed not to have noticed.

'Are you sure this is a wise investment, Laszlo?' cut in Davina. He turned to look at her, puzzled.

'Of course. I have every faith in Sophie's business intuition. Don't you?'

Davina did not answer. She was far too busy trying to restrain herself from slapping Sophie Ceretto's beautiful, serene, utterly irritating face.

Sophie was uncomfortably conscious of Laszlo standing much too close, his breath warm on her cheek. What's more, she was angry with herself for not being immune to him. Try as she might, she couldn't ignore the desire which smouldered within her when his hand brushed hers. But she would just have to learn to ignore it; at least, that was what she told herself as she politely but firmly escaped his touch and walked away.

Andre was beginning to believe that Sophie had been right all along. Business was picking up. Lady Anastasia Madeley was so pleased with her course of therapy that she had been recommending 'her simply darling therapist' to all her friends, and Stephanie Lace had been busy dealing with enquiries from potential new clients all week.

Nanette Duclos was one of the first to enrol on a course of treatment. She was petite but nicely rounded, French, very rich and wore her shiny black hair in a short, geometric bob which emphasised her fine cheekbones and full, naturally pouting lips. No one who looked at her would have imagined that this chic and vivacious Frenchwoman could have sexual problems.

'*Docteur*,' she breathed. 'It is so terrible! I cannot, no matter how I try . . .'

'Please, Nanette, don't worry. Worrying about it is half the problem,' explained Andre, sitting opposite her. 'If you get yourself into a state, it's hardly any wonder that you can't achieve orgasm.'

'You can help me, *Docteur* Andre?'

He patted her hand.

'Of course. Now trust me, and I will begin by helping you to relax.'

She responded easily, deeply susceptible to hypnotic suggestion; and this time he began to caress her, at first simply stroking her face and hair, then moving on to bolder caresses. This was her sixth session, and Andre had tried all his usual methods, to no avail. In all her thirty-one years, Nanette Duclos had never experienced an orgasm, and if he didn't try something more drastic, it looked rather as if she never would.

Normally Andre steered well clear of physical involvement with his patients – it was fraught with perils – but the experiment had worked beautifully with Lady Anastasia, and frankly he was running out of other things to do with Nanette. Besides, having sex with your patients was infinitely more pleasurable than listening to them going on and on about their dreams and their hang-ups.

'Can you hear me, Nanette?'

'*Oui, Docteur.*'

'Are you relaxed?'

'Relaxed. *Very* relaxed.'

'You feel warm, Nanette. Very warm. It's so hot in here. You want to take all your clothes off, isn't that right?'

'Yeees.' She gave a little sigh and wriggled about inside her Chanel blouse. 'May I take my clothes off, *Docteur*? *Il fait si chaud*!'

'You may.'

He watched with more than a flicker of interest as she peeled off first her blouse, then her very clingy skirt, writhing like a snake as she arched her back and pushed it down over her hips. Then the £500 Italian shoes, as carelessly discarded as the Reger brassiere and the tiny red panties.

Naked, her body radiated a luscious, somehow naive, appeal.

'You're beginning to feel lovely and warm, Nanette. Warm and cosy. There's a nice tingly feeling in your nipples. Isn't that right?'

'Oh yes.'

'Touch them. Feel how nice it is to stroke and pinch them. How does it make you feel when you touch yourself?'

'Lovely ... *tellement agréable* ... all warm and shivery, and oh, it aches in between my legs.'

'Touch yourself between your legs, Nanette.'

Her hand moved to the mass of black curls adorning her pubis. She seemed to hesitate.

'May I, *Docteur*?'

'Of course.'

'But ...'

'Is something wrong, Nanette?'

'No, *Docteur*, nothing is wrong, only ... would you touch me there? Please? I don't know how to do it properly. I'm sure it would feel much nicer if you did it for me ...'

He placed his hand upon hers.

'We'll do it together, Nanette. There, doesn't that feel good?'

He began rubbing her, very gently at first because he wasn't sure how she would react; but the hypnotic state had removed all her inhibitions, and almost at once she began moving her hips, pushing her pubis harder against his fingers. More daring now, he took her hand and insinuated it between her parted thighs.

'Rub your clitoris. Relax, Nanette. Relax and let it come. I'm going to make you come.'

Her response was quite astonishing. For years she had lain beneath her husband, moaning and sighing and doing everything she could to make him believe that she was enjoying herself; and now, for the very first time, she really was experiencing pleasure. There could be no doubt about it. Sweat was coursing over her naked body, her thighs were moist with the trickling, oozing juices from her flowering sex. And he could feel the hardness of her clitoris, swelling, distending, stretching itself out to meet their joint caresses.

'*Docteur, docteur, qu'est-ce qui se passe? Ah, ah, aaaah!*'

She collapsed forward and he had to catch her to prevent her falling, lowering her gently to the carpet. He could feel her heart thumping through the wall of her chest.

'You are perfectly relaxed, Nanette. Relaxed and happy. You feel good . . .'

'Good. Yes, yes, so good.'

'Now you will awake, but the pleasure will remain. And whenever you wish, you will be able to bring yourself to a climax again.'

He snapped his fingers. Nanette sank to the ground at his feet, panting and softly moaning.

'Are you all right, Nanette? Look at me.'

She raised her eyes to his. They were sparkling with an ecstatic light, the light of sudden revelation.

'*Docteur, docteur!* You have done it! You have made me well!' There were tears at the corners of her eyes as she reached out and took Andre's hands, covering them with kisses.

Faintly embarrassed by her enthusiasm, he drew his hands away.

'No, you have made yourself well. It was your own hands which brought you pleasure.'

'*Ah non, Docteur*, that is not true. It is you who have made me a woman, you alone. And I shall be grateful to you for ever . . .'

Stepping out of the shower, Sophie glanced at the clock. Almost nine-thirty. Time to get ready.

With Andre away at a conference and Stephanie and the housekeeper gone home for the night, she had the Hall to herself. She surveyed the clothes laid out on the bedspread, breathed in the scents of expensive lingerie and handsewn leather. A feeling of sublimely sensual exhilaration filled her, making her dizzy with anticipation.

Sitting down on the bed, she put on the red satin suspender belt and rolled on the black seamed stockings; seven denier Dior, soft and light as a whispered kiss. Then she bent forward and let her full breasts fall into the cups of the matching half-cup brassiere, which left her nipples so very immodestly bare and oh so enticing.

The gown was unusual to say the least. It had been individually designed to her specifications, with no expense spared, and Sophie knew even before she put it on that it was absolutely perfect. It radiated dominance, aggressive sexuality, sensual power.

She picked it up and stepped into it. The top part of the gown was of supple black leather, cut low in the neck and laced very tightly at the front. The boning was so subtle that it was quite invisible, yet powerful enough to cinch her waist to a tiny eighteen inches, and push her breasts upward and outward, like delicious offerings on some exotic salver.

The skirt of the gown was of scarlet watered silk, very full but slashed to the waist at intervals, so that if she turned suddenly it spun out like the petals of some unholy flower, revealing black-stockinged legs and scarlet spike-heeled boots, laced to the calf.

A pendant of diamonds and jet hung alluringly between her full breasts, pointing the way to a vale of perdition and pleasure. Oh, but it felt so good to be no one's slave, to play the dominatrix!

She caressed her body through the leather and silk. She felt alive, vibrant, incredibly aroused. Until now, she had not realised how dulled her senses had been without this dimension to her life. But how could she possibly have guessed that she would miss it, this life which she had so utterly rejected?

Reaching into a brass-bound trunk with scarlet-tipped fingers, she took out a pretty whip; thin coils of supple leather, intertwined with thin gold wire. Pretty, yes, but perfectly capable of dispensing discipline.

Her clothes rubbed deliciously against her body as she flowed down the stairs and out into the night. A limousine purred on the driveway, waiting just for her.

Before she stepped into the car, she took the invitation from her bag and read it once again: 'Decadence and Discipline: Emil Bernhardt invites you to a night of delicious debauchery.'

This invitation cost me enough, she thought to herself, *let's hope it turns out to be worth it.*

Chapter 4

'Clean. Lick it clean.'

Sophie's commands were quite precise, and to his credit her slave did try very hard to obey. His tongue wriggled as much as it possibly could, but it was a tall order to lick clean the very spike heel which was pinning it to the carpet.

'Imbecile,' sniffed Sophie, at last deciding that they had both had enough of this particular game. With a flourish of her scarlet boots, she walked away ... over her slave's prone body, causing him groans and sobs of exhilarated agony.

Glancing around, she saw that her little playlet had been observed closely by another of the partygoers, a tall and extremely good-looking man in his late thirties, dark-haired with eyes of piercing jet. He smiled as their eyes met, and she found herself responding. Gesturing to the Chief Constable still lying squirming at her feet, she explained, 'We used to know each other rather well when I was ... in business.'

'Indeed?'

'Oh yes. We had an arrangement. He would arrest me –

wearing his full dress uniform of course – and then later I would punish him for it.'

The handsome onlooker nodded, his mouth twitching into a lazy smile.

'A mutually beneficial arrangement,' he agreed.

Sophie pursed her beautiful scarlet lips and purred. This man made her *want* to purr.

'The best kind,' she declared.

'How very true.'

The stranger extended a strong hand in introduction. His voice held the faintest trace of an Australian accent, just exotic enough to be sexy.

'Emil Bernhardt. Welcome to my orgy.'

'Sophie Ceretto. Delighted to meet you, I'm sure.' She planted two chaste kisses on his cheeks, taking the opportunity to enjoy the warmth of his body, the firmness of the muscles beneath the tanned skin. Stepping back, she looked him up and down. 'Do I know you?'

He smiled.

'We've never met, but I know you.'

'How do you mean?'

'Let's say I know *of* you. Because of Marta Kolbuszewski. You were on her . . . "special" list.'

Sophie raised an eyebrow. For a moment, warning bells sounded in her head. The mention of Marta Kolbuszewski's name brought back too many uncomfortable memories.

They strolled together across the room, stepping over entwined bodies as they went. The scene was bizarre by anybody's standards. Now here was a man who knew how to throw a party, thought Sophie with some amusement.

Batman was rogering a Druid; two firemen were licking whipped chocolate mousse from between Cleopatra's thighs; and a man in a black rubber catsuit was massaging ice cream all over his naked cock and balls.

'You? You knew Marta? You don't strike me as the type who'd, you know ... *associate* with Marta ...'

This time Bernhardt laughed.

'To be honest I'm not, but in my line of work I often have to entertain important clients, and some of them expect something "unusual", if you get my drift.'

Sophie glanced across at the sunken bath, where naked men and women were rolling around in a slushy mass of crushed ice.

'Like that?' she suggested.

Bernhardt shook his head.

'Not quite. More ... one on one, if you get my meaning.'

Sophie allowed herself a knowing smile.

'As a matter of fact, I might just be able to help you there.'

Emil returned the smile. His eyes lingered a long time on her body, then travelled up to meet her gaze.

'I'm sure you will,' he replied.

Satin Miss was a perfectly respectable business.

You had only to walk past the old, beautifully preserved shopfront to see that it was an ordinary, if rather up-market, lingerie shop: the sort of place where a nice young lady might buy herself some luxurious underwear for that special occasion.

The only thing was ... ladies, young or otherwise, never entered Satin Miss. The only customers were men. And no underwear was ever bought and sold, only worn ...

And taken off.

Davina Templeton had found it difficult to adapt to her new position, in charge of the sales floor at Satin Miss. Being told what to do by Laszlo, she could accept without question. Being told what to do by Sophie Ceretto was a different matter. And the things she was forced to endure! The sights, the demands, the perversions she had witnessed ... She would have died rather than admit that some of them excited her, despite her prejudices and resentments.

She stepped out onto the sales floor at the precise moment when a customer entered the shop. He was a typical Satin Miss client, a middle-aged business type in a sober grey suit, set off with a Rolex and the odd bit of tasteful but expensive jewellery. Rich, not particularly memorable, yet undoubtedly powerful.

Davina switched on a smile.

'Good afternoon, sir. Can I help you?'

He glanced around the shop. The walls were adorned with exquisitely erotic lingerie – everything from fripperies of silk and lace to rubber, leather, PVC and even 'period' items such as stays, camisoles, open-crotch drawers and bust flatteners.

'Perhaps.' He met her gaze. 'Name's Smith.' (*What a surprise*, thought Davina.) 'I want to buy some lingerie for a ... lady friend.'

'Of course. Let me show you some of what we have. Did you have anything particular in mind?'

The beginnings of a faintly unpleasant leer crossed Smith's face.

'As a matter of fact, I do. She likes to dress up as a schoolgirl. Got anything suitable have you?'

'We have an extensive range of . . . unusual items. And anything we do not have, we shall be happy to have made to measure and delivered to you within three days.'

'I want to see it on before I buy it. You know, see what it looks like.'

'Naturally. If you'll just come through to one of the display rooms with me, you can select an . . . assistant to help you choose.'

Smith followed Davina through a door at the back of the shop, along a wood-panelled corridor and into Display Room One. Davina rang a bell and Indhira appeared.

'Bring the schoolwear items, would you? And ask the other assistants to come here. Mr Smith wishes to select one to help him . . . choose.'

'Certainly, Miss Templeton. Right away.'

Indhira gave a sly wink, but the customer did not respond, even though she was wearing the shortest of micro-skirts and the tightest of white silk bustiers. In fact, Smith seemed more interested in looking at Davina than at Indhira . . . and that was enough to make Davina feel curiously uneasy. She moved a little further away from him, hoping that Indhira would not take too long.

She reappeared with an armful of clothing, and followed by the other girls Sophie had selected at the Pink

Pearl. They were all wearing identical uniforms of short black skirt and tight white silk bustier, designed not only to display their figures to best advantage, but also to allow for swift undressing. Customers did not like to be kept waiting, as Sophie had quickly discovered.

'Would you like to select some items from these?' suggested Davina. 'Then you can choose an assistant and she will model them for you. In complete privacy of course,' she added, just in case the customer was a little shy. Not that he looked shy, she thought to herself. And he had still hardly taken his eyes off her body since he'd walked into the shop.

'This, this, this,' he grinned. 'Oh, and these.' He selected a complete school uniform of old-style gymslip, white shirt, striped tie, white cotton brassiere, black stockings and navy-blue knickers.

'And your choice of assistant?' Davina snapped her fingers and the six girls took off their bustiers, revealing the pleasing charms of their breasts. 'Which is it to be – Dee-Dee, Indhira, Vicky, Tas, Gunhilde or Jessamine?'

Smith gave them a cursory look, then shook his head.

'They don't interest me.'

'I'm sorry, Mr Smith, but these are our assistants. We have no others.'

He met her gaze.

'I want you.'

'What!' She felt her cheeks turn scarlet at the very thought of what he might mean.

'You heard. I want you to model them for me.'

'But . . . I'm afraid that's not possible. You see, I'm the

floor manager here, I don't . . .'

'Don't what?' enquired a cool voice behind her.

She swung round. Sophie Ceretto was standing in the doorway to the display room, looking – damn her – magnificent in a fitted suit of electric blue PVC, matched by spike-heeled shoes and glossy blue painted talons.

'What don't you do, Miss Templeton?' she repeated, walking into the room. Davina felt hot, cold and embarrassed.

'Mr . . . Smith isn't satisfied with our assistants. He asked if I would model the clothing for him. I explained that that wouldn't be possible . . .'

'Come outside, Miss Templeton. I wish to have a word with you. Please excuse us for a moment,' she added to the customer as they went out into the corridor, closing the door behind them. She leaned her back against the wooden panelling and folded her arms. 'What do you mean by refusing him, Davina?'

Davina gaped, for a few seconds unable to think of anything to reply.

'But . . . no way, Sophie, it's not my job. You and I both know that Laszlo only put me in here to help you with the business side. If you think I'm going to dress up and play the cheap tart for that revolting little man . . .'

Sophie smiled. 'The customer is always right, Davina,' she said quietly. 'Always.'

'No, Sophie. Uh-oh. Not a chance.'

'Do it, Davina. Do everything he asks you to, or I may have to have a word with Laszlo about the way you've been deliberately trying to make things difficult for me. Understand?'

For a moment, Davina thought about turning on her heel and storming out of Satin Miss for ever. Then she remembered that if she walked out on this she would be walking out on Laszlo too ... and Laszlo Comaneci was her one true obsession.

'Bitch,' she breathed.

'Thank you,' replied Sophie, and turning on her heel she left Davina to her fate.

Once back in her office, Sophie settled herself down in a comfortable chair and switched on the security system. There was a camera in Display Room One, which was incredibly convenient not only for ensuring that the clients didn't take any more liberties than they'd paid for, but also to make sure that the 'assistants' carried out their duties to the clients' *complete* satisfaction. Since it had opened, Satin Miss hadn't had a single dissatisfied customer, and Sophie had no intention of starting a precedent now.

My, my, she thought as Davina stepped into the room. She was dressed as a schoolgirl, her long legs showing black stocking tops under a short gymslip. Her brown hair was in pigtails, and her candy-pink lipstick was smeared across her generous mouth, giving her the appearance of an innocently wicked Lolita.

She listened as Smith called the shots. Davina was right of course, he *was* a revolting little man; but he had paid good money and was entitled to be revolting if he wanted to be.

'Bend over,' his gravelly voice commanded her.

With very bad grace, Davina obeyed; evidently not

quite to the customer's satisfaction, as he struck her a blow across the back of the legs with a ruler.

'Not like that – over the back of that chair. And pull up your skirt. I want to inspect your knickers.'

Up went the skirt, which Smith tucked into Davina's belt. Underneath she was wearing black stockings held up with elastic garters, and a pair of navy-blue uniform knickers – not on the face of it the most sexy of undergarments, but Smith was clearly transfixed by them. Sophie watched him run his hands over Davina's backside, squeezing and smoothing, exploring the consistency of the flesh through the thick blue cotton.

'You're a wicked girl. You've been having unclean thoughts.'

The ruler struck home again, this time across Davina's backside, making it leap into the air. She let out a startled, indignant cry.

'No! That's a lie!'

'How dare you call me a liar. I shall have to punish you for that.' Smith's voice was heavy with satisfaction, and Sophie saw that his cock was in his hand, a rapidly stiffening rod of flesh which might, perhaps, be the intended instrument of Davina's 'punishment'.

'Don't touch me!'

Davina's head flew up as Smith pulled down her knickers, baring the pale swell of her rump, marked now by a long red line where the ruler had struck it.

'Bend over, or I shall tie you to the chair and leave you there until you learn better manners.'

This time, Davina remembered what Sophie had

threatened and submitted to the indignity of her situation. Smith set about administering an energetic beating on her bare rump, until it had taken on the most delightful shade of crimson and seemed to radiate its own inner heat.

'Stand up and turn round.'

She did so with some difficulty, for her backside felt as though it were on fire.

'Take off your knickers, fold them up and place them on the seat of the chair.'

She did so, stepping out of the navy-blue horrors with an elegance which no one but Davina Templeton could have managed.

'Pick up your hockey stick. Hold it.'

Davina obeyed, clearly puzzled. She held the thing in her hands as though about to bully off for her House First XI.

'Not like that, you stupid girl. I want you to hold it between your legs.'

An expression of horror crossed Davina's face at the moment when she realised exactly what Mr Smith was demanding of her.

'I'll do no such thing!' she declared.

'Push the handle up your quim and fuck yourself, or I'll do it for you.'

This warning was enough to make her obey, though her face was set in a mask of distaste and her cheeks were as red as her backside. Sliding her feet apart, she braced herself against the chair back and slipped the handle of the hockey stick between her thighs.

'I can't . . . it's too big, it won't go in . . .' she protested.

One protest too many, mused Sophie, for at that moment Mr Smith's patience ran out and, taking hold of the hockey stick, he forced it deep into Davina's womanhood. The fact that it slid home with such obvious ease confirmed to Sophie what she had always known: that Davina Templeton's prudery was all a sham and that, deep down, she was a bigger slut than the rest of them put together.

Poor Davina, she thought to herself with just the faintest twinge of pity as Smith threw her to the ground and, with the hockey stick still wedged firmly in her sex, proceeded to take her from behind with unsophisticated enthusiasm.

But it was a *very* faint twinge of sympathy. Davina had made her life a misery for so long, and at last the tables were turning. No longer the slave, no longer the plaything of others, Sophie was beginning to enjoy herself.

There was a lot to be said for being in charge.

Andre and Sophie met up for lunch two days later, at their favourite brasserie. It was a kind of celebration lunch, though neither was quite ready to admit to the other just what they were celebrating.

Andre raised his glass.

'To success.'

Sophie met his gaze, smiled.

'To success.' She sipped her champagne. 'To us.'

Setting down his glass, Andre reached across the table and stroked the back of Sophie's hand.

'I haven't seen nearly enough of you lately. I hope you

haven't been bored, all on your own. Or am I flattering myself that I'm utterly fascinating?'

Sophie's blue eyes almost betrayed a flicker of guilt. What would Andre think of her if she revealed what she had been up to whilst he had been tending to his clients? What would he think if he knew that *she* had clients, too?

'I've missed you,' she replied with perfect honesty. 'But I've been . . . keeping myself busy.'

'Good.' He lifted her hand to his lips and kissed it. 'I feel terrible about neglecting you like this. But business has been picking up, and well . . . we need the money.'

'I'm glad the business is coming round,' smiled Sophie. 'Didn't I say it would?'

He pulled a face.

'Are you *always* right?'

'Always. So what are your new patients like?'

'Oh, you know. Most of them are boring rich people with not enough to think about. One or two are mad as hatters.'

'Are any of the women pretty?'

'A few.' Andre wasn't sure if he ought to feel guilty or not. He was a sex therapist, after all. But he did feel a bit guilty, even so. After all, most therapists employed surrogates to do their practical work for them; and, frankly, screwing Nanette or Lady Anastasia was more fun than it ought to be.

'And have you sorted out Lady Anastasia's little trouble?' she enquired.

'You know I can't discuss my patients' problems!'

'Not even with me?'

He kissed the end of her nose.

'Not even with you.'

And there are lots of other things I can't discuss either, he thought to himself. Like the excitement of pushing his dick between Lady Anastasia Madeley's breasts, or the peculiar pleasure of having Nanette Duclos running her pink kitten's tongue over his bare toes.

'Secrets, eh? How exotic. I wonder what you get up to in that consulting room of yours.'

'It's all very boring, really it is. Just a business.'

He wondered if Sophie believed him or not. She fiddled with her knife and fork, nibbled a little glazed chicken then took a sip of wine.

'Actually, I've decided to go into business myself.'

He raised an eyebrow.

'What kind of business?'

'A fashion shop. It's just an idea. I've been looking at premises with a friend of mine.'

'So that's what you've been doing. Can we afford it? Is it risky?'

She put her lips to his and transferred a sliver of chilled mango into his mouth. It tasted sweet yet sharp, spicy and honeyed and exotic.

'Just leave everything to me, darling. Don't worry about a thing.'

Andre growled his pleasure as Sophie filled her mouth with champagne and they kissed again, the chilled liquid swirling round their mouths, mingling with the stickiness of fresh mango and tingling with the tiny pinpricks of ice-cold fizz.

'People are beginning to take an interest in us,' observed Andre as he darted a trail of cold, sweet kisses down the smooth curve of Sophie's throat.

'Let them.'

'You like being watched?' His hand slid from her shoulder to her bare arm, then moved across to stroke the plump swell of her breast. 'I bet you'd love to do it right here, am I right?'

She giggled like a naughty schoolgirl, drew his head down and whispered in his ear.

'What colour panties am I wearing?'

'Black.'

'Wrong.'

'Red.'

'Try again.'

'I don't know . . . white?'

She dissolved into wicked, girlish laughter.

'I'm not wearing any.' She wriggled her backside across the seat of her chair. 'It's quite exciting, having all this scratchy moquette rubbing my bare quim. It makes me feel . . .' She winked '. . . you know . . .'

'Actually, I don't. Tell me.'

Sophie licked her lips. They were sticky and sweet with juice, just like the oozing well of her sex, which at this very moment was seeping its nectar into the red moquette of the seat cover.

'It makes me feel like I want to be fucked,' she enunciated, just clearly enough for the man at the next table to drop his spoon into his soup with a splash and a curse.

Andre wiped his hands on his serviette.

'That mango has made my fingers all sticky. I need to wash my hands. Care to join me?'

They got up from the table together, waving aside the waiter.

'We'll take coffee later,' said Andre. 'Much later.'

The waiter watched them walk across the restaurant together, towards the door marked 'Washrooms'. *Has he guessed what they were planning to do?* wondered Sophie. *Does his cock ache with the jealous desire to be in Andre's shoes?*

She felt exhilarated, twice as alive as she had felt until only a few days ago. What Andre didn't know couldn't hurt him, and Satin Miss was providing her with more than just the money they needed to keep Andre's business going. It was fulfilling a need she couldn't confess, not even to him. The need to explore a world of deep, dark, hidden sensuality. Now that she had found the way to satisfy her darkest desires, sex with Andre was a thousand times more exciting. At last she felt she could give and receive total pleasure.

The washroom door swung shut behind them.

'There's no one else here. Good.' Sophie reached out and bolted the door. 'Don't want any interruptions, do we?'

Floor-to-ceiling mirrors reflected every detail as Andre took Sophie by the waist and lifted her up on to one of the washbasins, easing her skirt from underneath her backside as he kissed her.

'So it's true – you really aren't wearing panties.' His hands explored the plump and gorgeous secret of her bare bottom. 'I didn't think you meant it.'

'I never lie.'

Perched on the washbasin, Sophie parted her thighs to welcome him in. Back arched, breasts thrusting into Andre's face, she took him deep into her moist womanhood, sighing with lust as his fingers worked their way into her secret haven.

Outside the washroom, someone was knocking politely on the door.

'Is there anyone in there? Are you all right in there?'

All right? thought Andre, sliding into Sophie until his balls were hard up against her backside. *This is better than all right. This is heaven.*

Chapter 5

Davina Templeton licked her lips.

Her hands were free, but she did not choose freedom. That was the last thing she wanted. Crossing them behind her back, she knelt down on the tiled floor. The highly polished black marble felt cold and seductive through her tight riding jodhpurs.

Laszlo's prick offered itself to her; it seemed huge, menacing, all-possessing. Ecstasy thrilled through her as she opened her ruby-glossed lips and encircled its head, engulfing it with infinite slowness.

Comaneci betrayed nothing of his pleasure as she began sucking and licking his shaft; Davina did not expect him to. He was her master, the only man for whom she had any respect, and positively the only one for whom she would willingly abandon everything at the snap of his fingers.

His penis was large and beautiful; many women had said so, but Davina told herself that she was the only one who truly knew the secrets to unlock his pleasure. She lavished kisses upon the glossy purple tip and was rewarded with a bead of clear, salty juice which welled up from the single eye at its centre.

She licked it up with relish, then another and another. He was weeping tears of joy, and *she* was the one who was making it happen. That alone made her clitoris throb with irresistible excitement.

'Suck it. Harder.'

His hand was on her dark brown hair, smoothing and twisting it, pushing her head down on his prick, making her do what she would have done willingly, a thousand times over. He filled her mouth, her throat, but she did not gag. She sucked greedily, taking every millimetre of lust-hardened flesh and still longing for more.

She felt him harden even as she sucked, the super-heated flesh turning to stone. But one fat blue vein on the underside of Laszlo's prick pulsed on, throbbing against her tongue, warning her of the inundation to come. She tightened her lips about the base of Laszlo's shaft, and worked them very slowly and tightly up to the tip, pausing to flick her tongue across the glans before moving slowly back down to the root.

Laszlo's self-control did not waver for a second. He made not the slightest movement, leaving it all to Davina. But she was a more than willing slave, and skilful too; and presently she felt him begin to quiver on her tongue. Delicious vibrations seemed to fill her being as his cock jerked, stuttered and spat, pouring its venom down her throat in a series of sharp, guttering spurts.

Heart pounding, she drank it down and Laszlo withdrew, wiping his prick clean on Davina's Chanel scarf – the one she wore because he had bought it for her.

'Very nice,' he said, putting away his cock and zipping it

into his pants. 'Now, what do you have to report?'

Davina felt irked to have to turn her thoughts to Satin Miss. She hated the place, despised it, truly she did. Not for the world would she have admitted how it turned her on to dress up in kinky underwear and play the little slut. No, no. Sluttishness was for those who really *were* sluts, like Dee-Dee and Tas – and Sophie Ceretto.

She sniffed.

'The business is doing well,' she admitted. 'I am keeping a tight rein on the management side. Sophie knows nothing about good financial control.'

The faintest flicker of a smile passed across Laszlo's face. He knew Davina's game, knew the mad jealousy in her passionate heart, knew how she'd love to scratch Sophie Ceretto's blue eyes out. It rather turned him on to be the object of such an overwhelming obsession. But, then again, since his path had crossed with Sophie's, Laszlo had learned a lot about obsession.

'Is that so? I seem to recall that Sophie knows a lot of other things, though.'

'Undoubtedly,' replied Davina. 'I am quite sure that working as a prostitute for Marta Kolbuszewski is excellent preparation for a career as a brothel-keeper.'

'If I want your opinions I shall ask for them. For the time being, I'd appreciate it if you'd confine yourself to the facts. Turnover is up?'

'Fifteen per cent on last month. Of course, without my specialist knowledge . . .'

'And there has been no trouble from the authorities?'

'None whatsoever. Which frankly surprises me.'

'Really?' It didn't surprise Laszlo. He had a lot of useful friends, some of them senior police officers. A word in the right ear could divert any amount of trouble. 'And the girls?'

'They seem ... competent enough at what they do.' Davina looked up at Laszlo. 'Can I get up now?'

He nodded. She got to her feet, watching Laszlo as he walked across to the office window and gazed out over the city.

'Is something wrong, Laszlo?'

He half turned to face her.

'As a matter of fact there is. Rick tells me that Trixie is still missing from the Pink Pearl.'

Davina shrugged. She was at a loss to know why a man as powerful as Laszlo Comaneci should bother himself with the disappearance of some sordid little showgirl with unfeasibly big tits.

'So?'

'So it causes me some concern.'

'But ...?'

Laszlo put up his hand.

'I want you to contact Zoë Mellenger.'

'At the detective agency? But why? Why bother?'

'Because I choose to. You will do it, is that understood?'

'Understood.'

'Good.'

Davina turned to leave, but before she had gone three steps Laszlo was standing in front of her, blocking the way.

'No, Davina.' Drawing her to him, he slid his hand underneath the waistband of her jodhpurs. 'You haven't quite finished your report yet.'

Sophie was on a business trip. To be honest it felt more like pleasure, but Amsterdam was absolutely *the* place to go if you wanted to find something exactly right for that special occasion.

The shop was situated not in some seedy backstreet, but halfway along a very respectable canal-side boulevard, tree-lined and prosperous. Sophie slipped the map into her pocket; she didn't need it. She knew exactly which shop she wanted.

She pushed open the door. Inside, the shop was an ultra-modern palace of chrome and dazzling white, set here and there with mirrors in irregular geometric shapes, and stylised but curiously indecent sculptures in wrought iron. Rail upon rail of clothes hung in discreet alcoves, tempting as baubles on a Christmas tree.

A young woman with cropped blonde hair came forward to greet her. Sophie didn't know her. She handed over her business card.

'Sophie Ceretto. From London. I have an appointment.'

The young woman checked her appointments book, nodded and smiled. Her voice was husky and lightly accented.

'Good afternoon, Sophie. I am Beatrix. I am here to take care of *all* your requirements.'

'I'm very glad to hear it.' And she was. Sophie appraised the young woman, her taut figure and long, athletic legs shown off by her white pencil skirt.

'Would you care to come through into our personal shopping suite? I can offer you a glass of wine while our models display our latest range.'

Sophie was led through into a room sparsely but comfortably furnished with two white leather sofas. The domed ceiling was almost entirely of glass, letting sunlight flood in, picking out a row of Pierre et Gilles photographs and a Hepworth sculpture of a reclining nude.

'We like to show our clothes here,' explained Beatrix. 'The ambience and the light are exactly right to show the fabrics off to best advantage.'

Sophie settled herself on one of the sofas and accepted a glass of red wine. She had spent several agreeable afternoons at the House of van Meer, but today she must concentrate on obtaining exactly the right outfit. Pleasure would come later.

'What type of outfit are you looking for?' enquired Beatrix. 'Do you have a price range in mind?'

'Money is no object. It must ooze sensuality, that is all I can tell you. I'll know it when I see it. *If* you have what I am looking for.'

'I am sure we can accommodate your needs, Sophie. Please relax, and I shall ask the girls to come in.'

The first of the models entered the suite. She was wearing a daring full-length gown of purple leather, the strapless bodice very tight beneath the breasts, which were left completely bare. The model's nipples were pierced, and linked by a silver chain which in turn was linked to cuffs of filigree silver about her ankles.

Sophie shook her head.

'Very nice,' she said. 'But too submissive.'

The second and third girls wore scarlet PVC, one in hotpants which bared her arse-cheeks through circular, transparent 'windows', her companion in a flimsy confection which was somewhere between a harness and a bathing costume.

'Too passé. I need to look . . . different.'

The fourth girl was dressed in a gauzy black bodysuit of sheer stretch nylon, over which she wore a short skirt of crimson tulle, very stiff and trimmed with silver beads which jingled as she walked. She was naked under the bodysuit, which revealed the beauties of her hard brown nipples and plump, shaven labia; and for a moment Sophie was tempted.

'This one?' enquired Beatrix.

Sophie hesitated.

'I . . . no. It is not quite right, somehow. Show me more.'

She was beginning to wonder if the House of van Meer was going to let her down when the next model stepped into the suite.

'That one!' she exclaimed.

'You are quite sure?'

'Absolutely. You can supply immediately?'

'Within a few days of taking your measurements. You will appreciate, it must fit very closely to the body . . .'

Indeed, thought Sophie, feasting her eyes on her chosen creation.

'I must try it on,' she declared. 'That is possible?'

'Of course.'

'You'll help me into it?'

Beatrix's grey eyes seemed to sparkle.

'I would be honoured.'

The black leather catsuit was delivered to her changing room within five minutes. Without even trying it on, Sophie knew that it was exactly right. It smelt right, felt right. She smoothed her fingers over the exquisite hand-sewn leather. This was it; an outfit in which she might play the perfect dominatrix.

Beatrix came up behind her, drawing the curtain so that they were quite alone, screened from prying eyes.

'You will allow me, Sophie?'

'Please – go ahead.'

Sophie's body tingled at the touch of a stranger's fingers, stripping away her clothes, unfastening her bra, helping her to step out of her panties and suspender belt. She glanced in the mirror. There was something rather deliciously indecent about being completely naked in a changing cubicle with a fully clothed and very beautiful young shop assistant.

Beatrix picked up the leather suit.

'First, a light dusting of talc – the leather must not chafe the skin. Now, if you could just slide your arms in here ... your foot in there ... that is exactly it. These straps must pass between your legs ...'

Initially, the leather felt cold and unyielding against Sophie's skin, and she wondered if she had made an unwise choice. But the warmth from her body seemed to soften and relax it, and as Beatrix pulled the suit up over her breasts it felt almost as if the leather was becoming a second skin, a part of herself, an outgrowth of her sensual soul.

'You would like it laced tight?'

'As tight as you can manage.'

She felt Beatrix's knee in her back as the Dutch girl pulled the leather laces tight, tighter, so tight that Sophie wondered how she was possibly going to be able to breathe.

'There, Sophie. You are quite ready now. Will you take a look at yourself in the mirror?'

Sophie stood back to gaze at her reflection. The black catsuit might easily have been made to measure, for it clung possessively to the curves of her body. It was cut very low at the front and back, just skimming the crests of her nipples; and was laced about the torso like an old-fashioned corset, emphasising her narrow waist and the ample swell of her breasts.

But the most distinctive feature of the suit was its silver fur trimming. It began as a high collar, encircling her throat, then snaked down and round her body like an amorous snake, sliding between her legs and then coiling itself down her right leg to the pointed toe of her boot.

Perhaps the most agreeable feature of all was the fact that beneath the fur trimming, the crotch of the catsuit was entirely open. The fur pressed against Sophie's pussy whenever she moved, tickling and exciting the sensitive flesh within.

Beatrix laid a hand on Sophie's arm.

'How does it feel?'

'It feels . . . delicious.'

'Those who have worn it say that it stimulates the body in a most delightful way.'

Beatrix's fingers stroked the side of Sophie's face. Sophie caught them and, drawing them to her lips, took them into her mouth. Beatrix let out a soft moan of pleasure, and when Sophie released her, she noticed that Beatrix's nipples were visible beneath her modest white blouse.

'Would you do me a further service, Beatrix?'

'Of course. Anything.'

Their eyes met, exchanging a silent message of lust.

'Go to the front door of the shop and turn the sign to "Closed". Then come back.' Sophie's fingers cupped Beatrix's breasts, feeling their ripe firmness. 'Come back quickly. I want you to help me get undressed.'

Andre was missing Sophie.

She'd only gone across to Amsterdam on some sort of shopping expedition – buying clothes for her new fashion shop or some such thing – but nevertheless he missed her. Even one night without her in his bed was one night too many. It didn't matter that Lady Anastasia Madeley was more than happy to console him; it was Sophie he wanted, and he ached for her. Just lately, sex between them had been better than ever, and when she got home he planned to give her champagne, a dozen red roses and the fucking of her life . . .

He glanced at the clock on his consulting room wall. Almost one-thirty. Getting up from his desk he walked out into the reception area.

Stephanie looked up.

'Doctor Grafton?'

'Do I have any more appointments booked in for today?'

Stephanie consulted the diary.

'No, Doctor. Nothing until Mr Mackenzie tomorrow morning.'

'Good. I think I'll get a bite to eat and take the afternoon off. If you need me, you can contact me on my mobile. Oh yes, and I've a couple of referral letters I'd like you to type.'

He went back into the consulting room to fetch the letters, and was on his way back to Stephanie when he heard a commotion outside. Hurrying back to the reception desk, he found Nanette Duclos, looking rather alluringly dishevelled and in floods of tears.

'*Docteur, Docteur*,' she sobbed, clutching at him.

'I tried to explain,' said Stephanie. 'But she won't listen, she says she has to see you right away.'

'Yes, yes, *Docteur*,' nodded Nanette. 'It is an emergency, I must see you now.'

Andre slipped his arm around Nanette's shoulders and flashed Stephanie a look which said, 'Make yourself scarce.' Stephanie was nothing if not discreet.

He led the sobbing patient into his consulting room and closed the door.

'Now, Nanette, whatever is the matter?'

She raised dark eyes which brimmed with tears.

'Oh, *Docteur* Grafton, *mon cher Docteur*, it is my husband . . .'

Andre took her by the arm and made her sit on the couch.

'Your husband? Has something happened to him?'

She shook her head vigorously.

'Not to Jean-Claude, *Docteur*, to *me*. I have changed, become ... sensual, a real woman. And my husband ...'

'He doesn't like the changes in you?'

'He does not approve. He says he finds me ... indecent.'

Nanette dissolved into tears again and Andre handed her a tissue from the box on his desk. He sat down on the edge of the couch, next to his patient, and stroked the back of her hand.

'Tell me everything.'

'I bought some new lingerie, like you suggested – a beautiful white basque and lace stockings – and I put them on and waited for him to come home. I called down to him from the bedroom ... "*Chéri, viens ici, je t'attends*." And he came up the stairs and saw me ... He called me a tart, *Docteur*, a cheap little tart who is no better than she should be! Now he will never be happy with me.'

Andre shook his head.

'That's not true, Nanette. Jean-Claude just feels insecure ... at the moment he is intimidated by your new sensuality. For so long you have been unable to respond to him, and suddenly you are the one making advances to him.'

Nanette left off sobbing and dabbed her eyes.

'If this is true, *Docteur*, what is it that I must do?'

'All you need to do is help him to find his own sexual release, as you have found yours.'

'But how?'

'I have an idea which might help you. Do you trust me, Nanette?'

'But of course, *Docteur*!'

'Completely?'

'*Mais oui*.'

'Good. Then come with me and I will show you what can be done.'

Taking her by the hand, he led her across the consulting room to the door which led to his private shower room. He clicked on the light.

'You're a very attractive woman, Nanette. You must never forget that.'

'You really believe so?'

'I know so.' He kissed her face, his hands roaming over her back and backside, exploring the petite beauty of her body. 'You will allow me to undress you?'

'This will help me, *Docteur*? This will help me to please my husband?'

'I am certain of it.'

A small sigh escaped from Nanette's lips as he began unbuttoning her sheer white blouse, then unzipped her skirt, letting its own weight drag it down over her hips and thighs. Underneath, she was wearing the white basque, g-string and white lace stockings which she had bought to seduce her husband. For a moment Andre felt a twinge of guilt, but he dismissed it; after all, this was his job. By showing Nanette how to give and receive pleasure, he was helping her to save her rocky marriage to Jean-Claude Duclos.

'Your body is exquisite, Nanette. Jean-Claude is a very lucky man.'

His fingers toyed with the straps of her basque. Leaning forward, he placed kisses on her throat as he slipped the straps down over her shoulders.

'Shall I take off my panties, *Docteur*?'

'No. Let me take them off for you. Close your eyes and imagine that I am Jean-Claude.'

She closed her eyes and her dark, curving eyelashes swept her creamy cheeks. Her lips were slightly parted, glossy with the wetness of saliva. Only a Frenchwoman could look so beautiful after weeping so copiously, thought Andre.

He reached down and slid his thumbs under the shoestring elastic of her lacy g-string. It was very, very skimpy, a tiny confection of white lace which left her small, round buttocks entirely bare, dividing them with a narrow thong. He pulled the g-string down over her hips, luxuriating in the smoothness of her waxed thighs, the wiry athleticism of her Gallic body. He wanted her, wanted her like crazy. An animal desire coursed through his veins, and it took every ounce of his self-control to prevent him simply throwing her down on the floor and ramming his cock up her wet and willing pussy. Sometimes, professionalism could be a real bind, he mused with wry good humour.

Nanette stepped out of her panties and Andre discarded them on the tiled floor.

'And my basque, *Docteur*?'

He shook his head.

'You look beautiful as you are . . . perfectly delicious.'

He ran his fingers down over the white satin cups in which Nanette's girlish breasts nestled so very temptingly, the boned corsage, the lace-trimmed margin which fringed the newly shaven mound of her pubis. Her inner labia pouted slightly from within the outer lips, protruding like the tip of a lewd and teasing tongue.

As Andre caressed Nanette's inner thighs, moving inexorably towards the heartland of her sex, she threw back her head and gave a shuddering sigh.

'Ah . . . ah, Jean-Claude, it is too much . . .'

Realising that he was overstimulating her too soon, Andre left off stroking Nanette's pussy and forced himself to hold back.

'You may undress me now, *chérie*,' he whispered.

She opened her eyes and stepped up to him, so that their bodies were touching, the points of her nipples pushing into his chest.

'You are beautiful, Jean-Claude. So beautiful, and I want you, I desire you . . .'

The heat of Nanette's passion communicated itself through her caresses, fumbling and urgent, her fingers desperate to unfasten Andre's tie, then his shirt, then the fly-buttons on his Armani flannels.

'Softly now, *chérie*. We have all the time in the world.' Andre was rather enjoying himself, playing this little scene. He could almost believe he really was Jean-Claude Duclos.

'*Non*, Jean-Claude. *Absolument non*. I must have you now, I can wait no longer.'

She practically tore his trousers off, and clawed at his jersey boxer shorts until they yielded, sliding down to reveal an achingly hard erection, wet-tipped and eager for her lips. Nanette caressed his balls with cool, subtle fingers.

'Come into the shower, *chéri*.'

He was more than willing to comply. Still dressed in her stockings and basque, Nanette kicked off her shoes and stepped into the shower, turning the water to hot and steamy.

'*Viens, chéri*, I am so ready for you . . .'

He joined her under the shower, entranced by the sight of the wet satin and lace clinging to Nanette's pert breasts, the dark crests of her nipples clearly visible now beneath the soaking-wet fabric.

'I am Jean-Claude,' he whispered. 'Show me how much you want to pleasure me. Suck me off.'

She slid to her knees in the shower, hot water cascading over her shoulders, turning her black hair to rats'-tails, steam swirling in clouds about her semi-nakedness.

It was paradise to feel her mouth close about his cock-tip, and his fingers scrabbled at the wet tiles, trying to keep himself from stumbling as pleasure weakened his muscles and sent his brain into a mad reverie of erotic delight.

'Suck me, suck me, suck me,' he heard himself gasp again and again. With each new exhortation, he felt Nanette suck a little harder, felt her sharp teeth grazing his flesh and the warm wetness of her muscular tongue winding and slipping over his iron-hard flesh.

His balls felt as though they were on fire: a great aching heaviness of burning lust hanging between his thighs. They seemed to contract suddenly, and all at once Andre was lost in a blind haze of ecstasy. He was dimly aware of Nanette's tight, wet throat, closing about his dick as he poured his tribute into her mouth; then a glorious warmth overtook him and he could scarcely keep himself from slumping to the floor.

Nanette licked the last drops of semen from her lips.

'Was that how I should do it, *Docteur*?' she asked, hanging on his every word.

He ran his fingers through her sodden hair, pushing the tangled mass back from her face.

'Oh yes,' he breathed. 'That was *exactly* right.'

That evening, Sophie left Satin Miss around eight o'clock and drove to the gym. It felt good to let go of the stresses and tensions of the day in a really punishing workout.

As luck would have it, there were few people in the gym that evening, and Sophie had the exercise machines to herself. An hour later, as she made her way back to the changing rooms, she heard a familiar voice calling her name. Turning round, she saw a tall, square-shouldered man with dark hair, standing in the doorway to one of the exercise studios.

'Sophie – how nice to see you again. I've missed you.'

'Emil! I didn't know you belonged to this gym.'

'There are lots of things you don't know about me yet. Why don't you spend a little time with me and find out some of them?'

She looked into Emil's dark eyes. They were enigmatic, giving away nothing of the mystery behind them. Sophie liked that in a man. She realised that, in a funny sort of way, he reminded her of Laszlo Comaneci. The same look of ruthless lust reigned in those dark eyes, the proud set of that handsome head.

He looked good, too; alluringly powerful in skintight exercise gear which left nothing to Sophie's vivid imagination.

'Do you think you have anything that might interest me?' she teased.

'Without a doubt.'

He stepped back into the exercise studio, and she followed him. It was empty, save for a set of parallel bars and a vaulting horse. Beyond the huge floor-to-ceiling windows, the London skyline glittered in the deepening dusk.

'I like to keep my body supple,' he commented as the studio door swung shut behind them.

'I can see that.'

'Of course, some kinds of exercise are even better for the body than others.'

'So I've heard.'

Her eyes searched his face. There was nothing in that expression but lust, there was no mistaking that fact, and Sophie found herself responding to the straightforwardness of his unspoken proposition.

'Let me show you round the equipment. The vaulting horse, for instance.'

'I'd like that.'

His strong hands took charge, bending her body over the horse, showing her how to stand, how to prepare herself.

'It's necessary to place the hands just here.' His hands were on hers, curling her fingers around the two leather-covered handles. 'Now arch the back just so . . . and thrust out the backside . . .'

She knew that this was no gymnastics' lesson, or at least not *that* kind of gymnastics. But that was just fine by her. She lent her body willingly to Bernhardt's insistent demands, pushing out her backside with lewd suggestiveness; wriggling her hips just enough to drive the man crazy.

He rewarded her with hungry caresses, stripping down her leotard and possessing her with a single, rough thrust of his dick. Sophie loved it; rejoiced in it; didn't care a jot if anyone saw them. All she wanted right now was the raw pleasure of a rough fucking. And Emil Bernhardt was just the man to give it to her.

Chapter 6

Sophie felt the sweet afterglow of Bernhardt's rough fucking for days. She simply loved to be taken like a bitch in heat, and Bernhardt had opened the floodgates of her sexual hunger. Its intensity was almost frightening. Somehow, deep in her subconscious, she knew that she had crossed an invisible Rubicon and would never be able to go back. Not, of course, that she would ever wish to.

There was Emil Bernhardt ... and there was Andre. But she *loved* Andre, and that was just it. She loved the whip and the cane, the harsh caress and the spike heel too; and she must make sure that her two worlds never met.

The immediate solution was to throw herself into work. Satin Miss was expanding, the word was out that it was the most wonderfully exclusive place for the discerning man – or woman – to have a good time, and Sophie was getting a fantastic buzz from the success of her business venture.

There was plenty of leftover leather in the stockroom at Satin Miss, and Sophie set her favourite designer to work, creating a whole range of risqué costumes for herself and her girls. There was unused space too, and Sophie set about using it, converting store cupboards and attics into additional 'consulting rooms' and 'modelling studios' where clients could relax and know that their needs were catered for with *complete* discretion.

Who could have thought that timid little Sophie Ceretto could make such a perfect dominatrix? Certainly not Marta, her one-time mistress, who had done her utmost to destroy Sophie and make her her slave. Now Sophie was the mistress, and she had an infinite number of willing slaves on whom to perfect her skills.

One afternoon, while Sophie was attending to a client in one of the new consulting rooms, Davina was obliged to seek her out to ask her advice on a problem. Normally Davina kept as far away from the consulting rooms as possible; after her experience with Mr Smith, she lived in mortal terror of being drawn into something which – horror of horrors – she might find herself enjoying. But the problem needed resolving urgently, and Davina had no choice.

She climbed the stairs to the second floor attics. That was the studio where Sophie was working – the third door on the right. She should simply have knocked and waited, but seeing that the door was slightly ajar, she was over-come by a sudden urge to spy on Laszlo's 'business associate'. Perhaps she would discover something that Sophie wanted to hide from her, something that she could use to turn Laszlo against her, so that she could have him all to herself?

Very quietly, she tiptoed up to the door and peeped in through the two-inch crack. What she saw within made her shiver with dark and guilty excitement.

Sophie Ceretto was in the middle of a *very* intensive training session. Davina knew that this sort of thing went on at Satin Miss, but up to now she had closed her eyes to it. Now she felt fear, fascination, anticipation ... and lust, guilty lust which she was powerless to suppress.

Sophie was dressed in nothing but a red PVC bustier and matching thigh boots with five-inch heels. She was squatting over the face of a chained and spread-eagled client, her buttocks spread wide and the man's eager tongue flicking in and out of her anus. As she masturbated herself with the blunt end of a bullwhip, Sophie exhorted her slave to ever-greater endeavours.

'Faster, slave.'

The slave responded with an incoherent moan, and Davina saw his tongue move faster, penetrating Sophie's arse even more deeply.

'I said faster. Or I shan't rub your cock with sandpaper, the way you like me to.'

Davina watched in horror-stricken fascination. She couldn't tear her gaze away. There was a terrible burning itch between her legs and it wouldn't go away, no matter how hard she tried to ignore it. Almost without realising it, she moved her hand to her crotch and began to rub it.

Sophie's backside rose and fell on her slave's face, making him bugger her with his tongue. This seemed outrageous to Davina; outrageous and disgusting and depraved. So depraved that she almost climaxed at the very sight of it. Rub, rub, rub. She couldn't keep her fingers away from her pussy. It was so very stimulating to see Sophie the dominatrix, wanking herself to orgasm over the ecstatic upturned face of some nameless slave.

No! Right on the very edge of orgasm, Davina realised what she was doing. No, for pity's sake, what was she thinking of? The shame of it, the shame of what this terrible place was doing to her. She had to get away, tell Laszlo she wouldn't stay here a moment longer.

But she didn't turn and walk away. She just stood there, her pussy aching, her desire whispering in her ear: *do it, you know you want to, do it, do it now*.

Sophie climaxed silently, her juices trickling down her thighs onto her slave's face. She stood up, the bullwhip wet and glossy with her nectar. Without turning round, she spoke; and her words made Davina shiver.

'Don't leave us, Davina. Now it's *your* turn to come.'

Andre was walking down a street on the smart side of town. It was a hot day, and even in his shirtsleeves he felt overdressed.

As he strolled along, thinking about nothing in particular, a girl walked past. Well, she didn't exactly walk past – it was more a case of wiggling. Hell but she knew how to move those snaky hips: they seemed to undulate inside her lime-green hotpants, which were cut so skimpily that the margin of her buttocks was clearly visible, peeking out of the legs of her shorts.

All of a sudden, Andre felt much, much hotter. He couldn't take his eyes off the girl – when all was said and done, he was flesh and blood and no red-blooded male would have been able to ignore six feet of supermodel in hotpants, white stilettos and the tiniest halter-neck top Andre had ever seen in his life.

She was slender, but with delicious touches of plumpness in exactly the right places. Her breasts were pert but full, the nipples upturned and the flesh delightfully mobile beneath the white cotton. Her thighs were slim but strong, and at the very top of the right one Andre made out a tiny tattoo of a Cupid, drawing his bow. A long plait of golden-brown hair trailed down her back like a mare's tail, swishing across the cleft between her buttocks.

Andre licked his lips. His throat was dry, his pulse racing, and there was an embarrassing bulge in his pants which he rather wished wasn't there – not in broad daylight, in a busy street.

He turned away, trying not to look at the girl; but they were headed the same way down the same street, and she was only a few yards ahead of him, swaying her incredible backside, leading him by the cock . . .

Without intending to, he began fantasising about the girl. What was her name? Jocasta? No, too cold and upper-class. Vanessa? Stuck-up and proud. Tasha, maybe, or Samantha. There was a wonderful combination of respectability and tartiness in that girl; she was so self-aware, so teasingly sexual even when she wasn't thinking about it.

What would she like him to do to her, if they were alone together? And how would it feel to strip off those skimpy summer clothes, and impose his lustful will on her?

He knew how she'd like it. Up against the wall, that's how. Up against the wall down some back alley, with her shorts down round her ankles and that creamy backside opening like a flower to his insistent cock. He imagined the coolness of her flesh against the volcanic heat of his erection, and his cock throbbed in his pants, hungry for release.

Up against the wall... with her pretty face pushed against the rough bricks and her breasts jiggling as he fucked her, long and hard. Or maybe another way: maybe doggy-style, on her hands and knees with her arse in the air. How he groaned at the thought of entering her, pulling her bum-cheeks apart and scything into her, possessing her, teaching her what you get if you walk down a street half naked, swaying your beautiful backside...

Snapping back into reality, Andre followed the girl to the next corner, rounded it... and found that she had disappeared. But how could she? Where could she have gone to? He looked around, puzzled. There was no one. Just an empty side-street and a sudden chill in the summer air.

He walked on a little further. He didn't recognise this street and he wasn't at all sure that he liked it. It was shadowy and he blinked in the half-light, trying to accustom his eyes to the sudden change.

There was no warning; he heard nothing – no footsteps, not a sound. But suddenly he felt something cold and sharp press itself insistently into the small of his back.

'What the ... ?'

He tried to struggle free, but the grip on his shoulder was strong and the sharp thing in his back suddenly got sharper. He winced.

'Bloody hell, what is this? You're hurting me. If it's my money you want . . .'

He heard laughter. A woman's laughter.

'You can never tell what will happen, Andre. What, or where, or when.'

'You – you *know* me?'

'Shut up and listen, Andre. You don't own your life, we do. And soon you'll have to pay to get it back.'

A woman's voice. *The* woman's voice? Surely not? Could the beautiful girl have been a decoy? Andre's mind raced. What the hell was going on – and was he going to get out of it alive?

The uncomfortable pressure in the small of his back vanished as suddenly as it had made itself felt. But he did not move. He dared not.

'Are you . . . still there?'

Silence.

'Answer me, for pity's sake! What is it that you want?'

After a very long time, Andre moved. Turned round. He was alone.

'Is something the matter, Andre?'

Sophie sat in front of the dressing table, putting on a diamante necklace. If Satin Miss continued to do well, perhaps this time next year she'd be wearing real diamonds.

'Something wrong?'

Andre paused in the middle of doing up his bow tie. 'No, nothing – why? Should there be?'

'It's just . . . oh I don't know, I can't put my finger on it really. You've just seemed a bit distant these past few days, that's all. You know, thoughtful.'

Andre wasn't quite sure what to say. He'd been very careful not to tell Sophie about what had happened to him in the street the other day. For one thing, he wasn't sure how she'd react to him following sexy young girls – and more important, the last thing he wanted to do was worry her. He was already doing enough of that for both of them.

He got up, walked across, kissed her on the back of the neck.

'Everything's fine, I told you. Never better.'

She flashed him a look which said 'maybe', then turned back to finish her make-up.

'Do I look OK?'

'Ravishing.' He chuckled. 'Correction: ravishable.'

His hands slipped down from her shoulders to her breasts.

'You're not wearing a bra.'

She smiled: that wicked, complicitous smile which only they shared.

'Actually, I'm not wearing anything under this dress, unless you count stockings and suspenders.'

Andre growled deep in his throat.

'Are you trying to make me burst out of these pants or what?'

'Down, tiger! We have to be at the party by nine-thirty, remember.'

Andre sighed.

'Do we have to go? We could have a party of our very own, right here in this room.'

'I wish we could. But I'm meeting a couple of business contacts there, and I thought you said Lady Madeley was going to be there too? You can't risk upsetting her, she's one of your most important clients.'

They arrived on the quayside just before ten. Sir Desmond Dukinfield's yacht was impressive by anyone's standards. It loomed up out of the darkness and seemed to go on for ever, the epitome of luxury.

Music blared out of the darkness, and it was obvious that the party was already in full swing. Couples were dancing on the deck, on the gangway, even on the quayside.

'Quite some party,' observed Andre, helping Sophie out of the car.

'Well, they do say Sir Desmond doesn't believe in doing things by halves. He has a wife, five mistresses *and* a gay lover.'

'Straight up?'

Sophie laughed and gave Andre a sly wink.

'Dunno. I've never asked him.'

She didn't add that Sir Desmond was one of Satin Miss's most prestigious – and free-spending – clients; nor that his special requirements were so special that of all her girls only Dee-Dee was prepared to put up with them. Still, at Satin Miss the customer was always right, no matter how peculiar he might be, and tonight Sophie intended spreading a little goodwill among Sir Desmond's friends and business associates. The business could do with more customers who had eight-figure bank balances.

They walked together up the gangway and on to the

yacht, where a gorilla in a white tuxedo scrutinised their invitations before grudgingly letting them pass.

'Security's tight,' observed Andre.

'Yeah, well, someone tried to kill Sir Desmond last year, don't you remember? A jealous ex-lover or something, I can't quite remember. He was in hospital for a week with stab wounds.'

'Oh . . . yeah.' Andre felt a cold shiver run down the back of his neck.

'Is something the matter?'

'I'm fine. Well, we're here now, what next?'

Sophie stood on tiptoe and kissed him, her hands roaming over his body so discreetly that not a soul noticed her rubbing Andre's cock through his pants.

'I think we should split up for a while – you know, mingle a bit. I've got my two clients to see, and it wouldn't do you any harm to butter up the Madeleys – maybe they've got a few screwed-up friends who could use some therapy.'

Andre wasn't particularly happy about this arrangement, but Sophie was right; they both had businesses to think about, and it looked as if Sophie was really making a go of her lingerie shop.

He watched Sophie disappear towards the bar with a couple of businessmen, then took a drink from a tray and made inane conversation with a bunch of nobodies for what seemed like ten hours but couldn't have been more than a few minutes.

The sight of a familiar face made him sigh with relief. Lady Anastasia Madeley was heading straight towards him, a champagne cocktail in her hand and a smile of welcome on her scarlet lips.

'Andre, *darling*! How lovely to see you. Excuse us won't you? We have important business to discuss.'

She drew him aside.

'I hope you don't mind me stealing you away from your friends, Doctor Grafton.'

He laughed.

'Hardly. Ten seconds longer with that lot and I'd have turned into an axe-wielding psychopath.'

'In that case it sounds as if mine was a mission of mercy.'

'Oh definitely.'

He joked easily enough, but Anastasia Madeley was not a stupid woman.

'Andre, darling?'

'Hmm?'

'Is there something wrong?'

'Why – do I look ill or something?'

'Not ill. Distracted, I suppose. As if there's something on your mind. Would you like to talk to me about it?'

He smiled and wagged his finger at her.

'I thought I was supposed to be the therapist around here.'

'And so you are. But even a doctor needs a little healing sometimes.' She moved closer to him, so that their bodies were touching and he could feel the heat of her body, flooding into him through his thin summer jacket. 'You've been so good to me, Doctor Grafton; you've really helped me over my ... you know ... difficulties. Won't you let me help you?'

She slipped her hand inside his tuxedo, and ran it slowly and lasciviously over his belly and chest.

'You're so tense,' she murmured. 'I could help you relax.'

Andre hesitated. This was, after all, the middle of a party and not the comforting privacy of his consulting room. On the other hand, he had been aching for release ever since watching Sophie getting dressed; and what was more, he didn't want to be alone. Since that experience in the street, he found he didn't enjoy being on his own at all. The warmth and comfort of Anastasia Madeley's touch was just too much to resist.

'Let's go get ourselves a little privacy,' he suggested.

He'd never been on a yacht this size before, but Andre had a hunch there had to be one or two secluded cabins somewhere below decks. Anastasia followed him down the companionway, in and out of groups of laughing, chattering guests, and into the relative quiet of a semi-deserted corridor.

'Here?' She pouted teasingly at Andre. 'Where everyone can see us? I didn't realise you were quite so adventurous.'

He grimaced.

'I'm not. Let's see if we can find a cabin or something.'

The first door opened on to a cupboard; the second and third on tiny cabins which already housed writhing bodies. It was hard to tell how many in the half-light – all Andre could make out was a jumble of naked arms and legs, with here and there the odd breast or buttock, white and plastic-looking in the occasional flash of coloured light which reached down here from the deck above.

Anastasia peeped in and giggled.

'How *naughty*!' she whispered delightedly. Her fingers found the crotch of Andre's pants and started rubbing his semi-erect dick through his pants. 'Will you be naughty with me, Doctor?'

Quite frankly he would have liked to push her into the room, throw her down on the floor and have her right there and then. But he'd never been particularly into group sex, and the thought of all those heaving, groaning bodies rolling around on the floor took the edge off his ardour. Gently and very reluctantly he took her fingers from his dick, kissed them and closed the cabin door.

'Let's try next door. They can't *all* be booked for mini-orgies.'

The third door they tried opened not on a cabin, but a huge and opulent stateroom. Andre clicked on the light and whistled his appreciation. The room was lined with oak panelling, designer leather settees and a set of Modiglianis which were just too damn vibrant to be anything but the real thing. The centrepiece was a vast heart-shaped bed covered in red satin. It was hideous. It was tasteless. It was perfect.

'Here?'

He felt a grin take over his face. 'Here.'

'What if Sir Desmond . . .?'

'He won't.'

Just to make sure they weren't disturbed, Andre propped a chair underneath the door handle. They were alone at last.

'This must be where Sir Desmond brings his lovers,'

observed Lady Anastasia, sitting down on the edge of the bed and smoothing the flat of her hand over the satin bedcover. It made a swishing sound, low and sensual.

'I'm sure he won't mind lending it to us for a while.'

Andre felt emboldened and very, very horny. He sprang like a tiger, pushing Anastasia back on to the bed. They sprawled there together, laughing helplessly.

'Beast,' she enunciated with aristocratic precision.

'Do you want me to stop?'

'Don't you dare. This is part of my treatment – you have to do exactly what I want, or I shall have a relapse.'

'And what *exactly* do you want, Anastasia?'

'I want you to fuck me.'

Which was a happy coincidence, thought Andre, seeing as that was exactly what he wanted to do to her.

He tore at her clothes, fumbling for the zipper and managing to drag it down. Anastasia seemed not to care that he was clawing at her £2000 gold Versace gown; she was too busy tearing off Andre's trousers and pulling him down on top of her.

Animal sex, that's what this is, thought Andre; *and it's wonderful – raw and rough and comforting*. They didn't even bother getting properly undressed. He just pulled down the top of Anastasia's gown to bare her breasts so that he could suck on her nipples whilst he pushed up her skirt and fucked her.

Nor did he bother taking off her panties. He just pushed aside the crotch and plunged into the moist, warm honeypot of her quim. She tightened instinctively about his member, imprisoning him ... but he was a happy prisoner. He didn't want to escape from Anastasia's embrace, not now, not ever.

While he was on top of her, ramming his cock into her, fucking her to the mad rhythm of their mutual hunger, he could lose himself in the quest for pleasure. He didn't have to think about crazy women with knives, whispering dark menaces he didn't even understand.

She was hot, wet and ravenous for him. Thirty seconds after she had sucked the jism from his balls, she was on him again, pushing him on to his back and wanking him back to hardness with an almost brutal eagerness. It would have been impolite to refuse her, and he submitted to her ministrations with a smile on his face. Really, it was quite remarkable what skills resided in those slender, aristocratic fingers and their sharp, gold-varnished nails.

Anastasia sat on his prick with dramatic suddenness. He shuddered and grabbed great handfuls of her buttocks, forcing her up and down, using the wet sheath of her sex to wank himself to a second, and far more powerful, orgasm.

He licked his come from her thighs, moving up to dart his tongue into her sweet, slippery well. She sighed and arched her back, opening her thighs very wide to welcome him in; and he felt an electric thrill pass through her as he licked her to a climax.

They lay together for a few minutes, their hot bodies cooling on the dampened satin.

'You're good,' murmured Anastasia. 'Very good.'

His fingers walked over her sweat-sticky skin. He felt high as a kite, tripping on great sex.

'Glad to be . . . of service.'

Anastasia laughed as she rolled over and sat up.

'I prescribe another course of the same treatment, very soon.'

Andre reached out and picked up his discarded shirt.

'Perhaps we'd better go. Before Sir Desmond discovers we've been taking advantage of more facilities than he bargained for.' *And before Sophie notices that I've disappeared*, he added to himself. He didn't feel exactly guilty about what he and Anastasia had been doing but, if push came to shove, explaining could be a bit of a bitch.

They dressed as though they were two strangers who just happened to have found themselves naked in the same room. They did not touch or kiss – now that passion had been sated, touching seemed an irrelevance.

Removing the chair from underneath the door handle, Andre stole a glance outside.

'There's no one about. Let's go.'

'Perhaps we should leave separately?'

'No need.'

They stepped out into the corridor, Andre tucking his shirt into his trousers. He hoped he didn't look as dishevelled as he felt. But at least no one was around to take an unhealthy interest in what they'd been doing.

No one – and then the door to one of the washrooms opened and a woman walked out. Andre stiffened. *Oh shit, not her, not here.*

Nanette Duclos turned to walk back up the companionway. She could hardly have failed to notice Andre Grafton and Lady Anastasia Madeley, emerging together from Sir Desmond Dukinfield's stateroom. Nor did she fail to take in Andre's crumpled shirt, or the look of complicity which passed between him and Lady Madeley.

Andre and Nanette studied each other in silence for a couple of seconds.

'Good evening,' said Andre at last, desperate to break the tension of silence.

'Is it?' snapped Nanette drily, and she turned and walked quickly away.

'Touchy bitch,' remarked Anastasia. 'I don't expect she's getting enough.'

But Andre knew it wasn't that. He'd seen the look in her eyes – and it was a look of pure, venomous jealousy.

Chapter 7

A fierce white light glared menacingly through the slats of a black Venetian blind, reflecting coldly off the bare, distempered walls. A line of steel bedframes had been pushed up along one side of the room. The air was filled with the smell of disinfectant and stale piss. Sophie nodded her approval. This was definitely the best 'hospital ward' she had ever created.

And what a strange ward it was, she thought to herself. A ward whose equipment was tailored to the very specific requirements of its inmates.

The ward had several patients today, each one occupying a bed designed to meet his very individual needs. There was Mr Qalifa, strapped down naked on a bed of nails; Mr Benson, his bare flesh encased in sheets woven from rough, abrasive horsehair; Mr St John, transported by an angelic smile as white-coated assistants turned a heavy wooden handle, tightening the rack on which he lay.

Leather matron Sophie Ceretto took a glance at her reflection in the back of a highly polished bedpan. Her garb was a mockery of a nurse's uniform made entirely of white leather, slashed in strategic places to reveal tantalising glimpses of bare flesh. Her white, high-heeled boots tapped ominously on the tiled floor as she set out on her daily rounds. Her assistants, Indhira and Tas, followed her with a hospital trolley laden with all the necessary equipment.

She stood beside Mr Benson's bed and snapped her fingers. Indhira handed her a chart.

'Has he been receiving the prescribed treatment?'

'Yes, Matron. Enemas twice daily as you instructed.'

'No penile manipulation?'

'No, Matron. Your instructions were very strict . . .'

'Quite. Pull back the covers, I wish to take a closer look at my patient.'

Trudy stripped back the white sheet. Underneath, Mr Benson was entirely swathed in a horsehair blanket. His body twitched almost continuously as he wriggled in the grip of a terrible torment. Sophie knew perfectly well that the scratching of the horsehair both tortured and stimulated him.

'Matron . . .' gasped the patient. 'Please . . .'

'You *will* be silent, Mr Benson,' Sophie commanded him with all the sternness she could muster. 'Your treatment has scarcely begun, and your disorder is very severe.'

'You *must* put your trust in Matron,' agreed Indhira. 'Matron knows best.'

Sophie nodded to Indhira, who unwrapped the blankets from the patient's body. The horsehair had done its work well, leaving Benson's body covered in bloody scratches.

Sophie noticed with pleasure that his penis was stiffly erect, despite the fact that it was scratched and swollen from its martyrdom.

She peered closely at his genitalia, as though making a learned diagnosis.

'His testes appear to be rather engorged,' she observed. 'Turn him onto his belly, I wish to perform a rectal examination.'

She felt the shivers of excitement run through Benson as he was lifted and turned, quite roughly, on to his front. His backside was scratched and bruised from the 'medicinal' beatings which he had received as part of his very expensive course of treatment.

Sophie reached out a hand and Trudy stepped forward with a kidney bowl, covered with a crisp green cloth. She whisked it off. In the bowl lay a black rubber glove, covered with moulded spikes.

Sophie slipped the glove on her right hand.

'Prepare the patient.'

Trudy held Benson's buttocks apart, and Sophie pushed her index finger into his anus. He swallowed it up eagerly, thrusting his backside out to accept the spines which clawed at the sensitive membrane. Sophie chastised him by slapping him with her left hand.

'You will not move. You will lie completely still and take your medicine.'

This time he obeyed, but his entire body was quivering as the second and third fingers slipped into his arse. She kept him on the edge for a while – after all, he had paid good money to come to her for 'treatment', and would not take kindly to it all being over in an instant. But there was a limit even to her skill . . . and her cruelty. She felt for his prostate gland and squeezed it, long and hard.

Benson let out a long scream of agony and squirted his jism all over the horsehair blanket.

'Tut, tut,' observed Trudy. 'The patient has wet himself. What treatment do you prescribe, Matron?'

Sophie considered for a moment.

'Two-hourly ice baths, followed by applications of hot mustard infusions to the testes. Next patient, Indhira.'

They moved on from patient to patient, Sophie dispensing her unique brand of sexual medicine, until they reached the final patient. Mr Qalifa was a wealthy arms-dealer from Bahrain, a man who gained his pleasure from sampling some of the pain his stock in trade inflicted on others. Sophie despised him – which made it so much easier to enjoy punishing him.

She surveyed him, lying naked on his bed of quite blunt six-inch nails. He was a rather heavy man, and their tips had drawn blood in places, but Qalifa seemed not to mind. On the contrary, he seemed to be floating in an ecstatic reverie. This would not do!

'Your report on this patient, Nurse Gupta?'

Indhira stepped forward.

'The patient enjoyed a troubled night, with two seminal emissions.'

'I see. So we have not yet succeeded in overcoming his problem with overstimulation of the sex glands?'

'No, Matron.'

'Then we must increase the level of stimulation. Mr

Qalifa must learn to discipline his sexual response.' She searched her extensive repertoire for a suitable torment. 'You may apply sandpaper to his glans.' She flashed Indhira a meaningful look. 'And make sure you do it really *hard*.'

It was a strange life, thought Sophie to herself. But an enjoyable one, for all that.

In a vast hothouse, the size and style of something you might expect to find in Kew Gardens, a dark-haired man was picking his way through a man-made jungle.

Brightly coloured parrots and birds of paradise took flight as he pushed through the dripping foliage. Somewhere in the distance, a waterfall was cascading down a twenty-foot-high jumble of rocks, into a deep pool of warm and steaming water. Evidently the creator of this self-contained paradise did not believe in doing things by halves.

Forcing his way through a tangle of lianas, he found himself in a small clearing, where an older man was enjoying the attentions of a Swedish masseuse. He was lying face-down on a patch of soft, warm earth, whilst she kissed and nibbled the swell of his bare arse. At the dark-haired man's approach, he turned.

'I wondered where you had got to.'

'I was held up. A small business hitch, nothing more.'

'I trust that it is nothing that will impede our plans coming to fruition?'

'Not at all, I assure you.'

'And it will happen soon?'

'Everything is in hand.'

'Good.' Pushing away the masseuse, he sat up. 'In that case I suggest you stay here a while and enjoy the facilities whilst we discuss our business plan.' He clapped his hands. 'Which would you prefer – a blonde or a brunette? Or shall I order you both?'

Andre leaned back in his chair and placed the tips of his fingers together. This, without a doubt, was one of the most unusual problems he had dealt with in a long time.

'Go on,' he said. 'I think you'd better tell me all about it, don't you?'

Jake Priestley, more commonly known as the Black Count, shifted uneasily on the consulting room couch. Coming to see Doctor Andre Grafton was very much a desperate measure for him, and he wouldn't even have considered it if he hadn't had it on personal recommendation that the good doctor was effective, broad-minded and very, very discreet.

'I have this fantasy,' he said, his throat dry with emotion.

'Go on.'

'I get married to this really normal girl – you know, blonde, slim, pretty. We buy a house in the country and have two nice kids. And I get a job, you know, a real job. An accountant or something. Something incredibly boring . . .'

'I think you'd agree that this is unusual,' ventured Andre. 'For someone with your lifestyle . . .'

Jake gave a grunt of exasperation.

'Look, I never wanted to be a black-metal star, OK?'

'Then why . . .?'

'I was just a kid, all that satanism stuff seemed like a bit of a joke. We got a band together, got a bit of a name for ourselves, munched the heads off a few rubber bats, and the next thing I know, we've got ourselves a recording contract. That was five years ago, and now I'm a bloody underground cult. Have you any fucking idea how that feels?'

'Not really,' admitted Andre. 'But I imagine you must feel there is a lot of pressure on you.'

Jake gave a humourless laugh.

'Pressure! Look, man, you don't know the half of it. I'm trapped, there's no way out – being the Black Count is the only thing I know how to do, the only way of making money. But it's really getting to me. The fans . . . they think they know me. Some of them are totally out of their heads on black magic and God knows what. And the women . . .'

Now we're getting to the heart of it, thought Andre.

'Tell me.'

'We were playing Germany and there was this girl . . . Virna, she said she was called. She turned up backstage one night. Turns out she'd hitched five hundred miles to see me.'

'What's so unusual about that?'

'Unusual? Nothing. Except that she's a virgin, and she's been saving herself – for me. She's only come to the gig because she wants me to ritually deflower her in a cemetery!'

Andre looked up from his notes.

'And you felt pressurised to be what she wanted you to be?'

'Yeah. Yeah, I guess that's right. The other guys in the band were egging me on, and we'd all dropped a little too much acid. Next thing, it's pitch black and I'm freezing my bollocks off in some German boneyard . . .'

Andre waited for him to go on. He saw that Jake was clenching and unclenching his long, white fingers. He looked to be a pretty scared, screwed-up, young man underneath the black leather and gothic eyeliner.

'She was *really* crazy, man. Turned out she was into this black magic stuff like you wouldn't believe. She wanted me to throttle a chicken and make her drink its blood. And pain – she wanted me to really hurt her; you know, tie her naked to a gravestone and whip her, and only fuck her when she was half-dead.'

Andre asked the question which he knew Jake didn't want him to ask.

'And did you?'

The silence was as eloquent as Jake's reply.

'Yeah.'

'How did you feel about it.'

'I . . .' Jake clammed up.

'Please, Jake, you have to go on. How can I help you if you don't tell me everything? You mustn't hold back.'

'I . . . it turned me on. You know, *really* turned me on. Too much. I nearly killed the kid, and d'you know what's worse?'

'What?'

'She *thanked* me for what I did to her. Practically fell down and worshipped me.' He wiped his hand across his sweating brow. 'You have to help me, Doctor. Things are getting scary. I don't think I can control myself any more. It's like I'm living in a nightmare. It's got so bad, I can only get a hard-on if I'm thinking about pain.'

Andre put down his pen.

'OK, Jake. I can help you.'

Jake sat up and swung his long, thin legs over the side of the couch.

'No kidding, Doc? You really think you can get me out of this mess I've got myself into?'

'Oh, I can definitely help you, but you're going to have to help yourself too. That means complete honesty, you understand what I'm saying?'

'Yeah, I guess so.'

'I shall need to know everything about your sex life, and that means everything.'

'Sure. No problem. But how long is this going to take?'

'I don't know. Maybe weeks, maybe months. This is only your first consultation, it will be easier to tell when we've had a few more sessions.'

'Is that it then?'

'For today, yes.'

Jake reached into the pocket of his leather trousers and pulled out a roll of banknotes. There must have been a couple of thousand, at least. No wonder the black Count was finding it so difficult to give up the music business. Andre waved the money aside.

'If you see my receptionist, she'll sort everything out.'

He ushered Jake to the door. 'Make an appointment for a week's time.'

He was writing up Jake's notes when Stephanie buzzed him on the intercom.

'What is it, Steph?'

'There's a message for you, Doctor. A letter. Shall I bring it in?'

'Yes, fine.'

Stephanie handed him the envelope. It looked ordinary enough, but something held him back from opening it until she had left the consulting room.

He took the letter knife and slid it along the top edge. Inside was a white card, perfectly plain except for a small pink heart, a time and a location.

Deep down inside, Andre knew that it was stupid to respond to the card. It could be from anyone. He should just tear it up and throw it in the bin – or maybe even hand it to the police, and tell them what had happened to him that menacing afternoon in the street.

Of course he had done neither. He had slipped the card into his pocket and was waiting in the market square at precisely two o'clock in the afternoon, exactly as the card had instructed.

He waited. Shuffled from one foot to the other. Thought about turning round and going home before Jeremy Beadle popped out from behind a lamppost.

At that precise moment, a long black limousine with tinted windows drew up alongside the kerb. The driver's door opened and a chauffeur stepped out – the most

122

glamorous chauffeur Andre had ever seen, tall and blonde and very definitely female.

'Doctor Grafton?'

'Yes.'

'Please get in.'

She opened the rear passenger door but Andre hesitated.

'Where are we going?'

'I'm sorry, I can't tell you that.'

Heart thumping, he got into the car. The chauffeur closed the door behind him and the limousine moved off. Almost immediately he regretted it. What the hell had he got himself into? Why hadn't he been sensible and thrown the card away?

Well, it was too late to change his mind now. He surveyed his surroundings. The interior of the car was the height of luxury: white leather seats, brass and walnut trim, a bottle of champagne in an ice bucket at his elbow ... and a small colour television which flickered suddenly into life.

Intrigued, he leaned forward. There was, after all, nothing else to look at. The driver's compartment was blocked off with solid walnut and the windows were so heavily tinted that he couldn't see a thing on the outside. What was that on the screen? The fuzziness cleared and a message flashed on:

'RELAX, ANDRE. MAKE YOURSELF COMFORTABLE.'

He caught his breath as the message gave way to pictures. Pictures from a video camera, slightly out of focus but quite clear enough for him to identify one of the two figures on the screen. It was Sophie! Sophie in a black leather catsuit trimmed with fur. Sophie sitting on a naked man's face, wanking herself with the end of a bullwhip.

Before he had a chance to get over the shock of the first sequence of pictures, the scene changed. It was Sophie again. Sophie walking into her shop, Satin Miss. Walking past the rails of lingerie, up some stairs and through a door into a room done out as a sort of crazy hospital ward. There were men lying on beds of nails, tied to medieval-looking racks, bound and gagged and chained. And Sophie was dressed as a parody of a hospital matron, fisting one of her 'patients' . . .

Image followed image. Sophie was not in all of the film clips. Some showed other faces he vaguely recognised – girls Sophie had introduced to him as 'customer advisers' from the lingerie shop; then one or two he vaguely remembered as dancers from the Pink Pearl.

Suddenly the pictures stopped, and another message flashed up:

'OH DEAR, ANDRE. HOW WOULD IT LOOK IF PEOPLE KNEW?'

The scene switched abruptly to one which Andre recognised only too well. A shudder of cold horror ran over his flesh as he watched himself cavorting with Lady Anastasia Madeley in the stateroom of Sir Desmond Dukinfield's private yacht. Others followed: clip after clip in which he took a more than professional interest in his female patients. Then the same message again:

'HOW WOULD IT LOOK IF PEOPLE KNEW?'

A pause, a blank screen, then:

'THEY WON'T. NOT IF YOU COMPLY.'

A sound made Andre look down. A small hatch opened in the partition between the driver's and passengers' compartments, and as he watched a package fell through on to the floor at his feet.

He picked it up. There was a tag attached to it. It read: 'FILL THIS WITH MONEY. LEAVE IT IN THE POSTBOX ON MADISON GROVE AT THREE O'CLOCK ON WEDNESDAY AFTERNOON. OR TAKE THE CONSEQUENCES.'

At that moment the limousine ground to a halt and the door opened. Clutching the package under his arm, Andre stepped out on to the pavement. He found himself at exactly the same spot where he had been standing when the car arrived. Just as he opened his mouth to ask the driver what the hell was going on, she accelerated away from the kerb, leaving him alone with his thoughts.

Chapter 8

The police surgeon folded his arms, contemplating the broken glass phial and the empty whisky glass.

'If you ask me it was suicide,' he announced.

Detective Sergeant Aubrey glanced up from his notebook.

'We're quite sure of that, are we, sir?'

'No question about it. There's enough horse tranquiliser in here to knock out the Household Cavalry. Admittedly there's no suicide note . . .'

'Yeah, well, there hardly ever is, except in episodes of *Inspector Morse*. My suicides don't tend to be that considerate. Anyway, from what I hear the deceased had big money worries.'

'That settles it then. Get someone to ring the coroner, would you? There's a mountain of paperwork to process before we can release the body. I take it there's a widow?'

Aubrey nodded.

'Yeah. Well, a live-in lover. Name of Sophie, Sophie Ceretto.'

The police surgeon folded his stethoscope and put it

away in his black bag. Taking a rather nice Schaeffer pen from his top pocket, he proceeded to scribble on a notepad.

'Time of death, somewhere between eight p.m. and midnight. Cause of death, massive cardiac and respiratory failure due to self-inflicted barbiturate poisoning. Name, Doctor Andre Peter Grafton.' He handed the death certificate over. 'Here you are, Sergeant.'

'Thanks.' The detective shook his head. 'Never bloody learn, do they? Take the coward's way out and leave everybody else to clean up the mess.'

A week later, with the inquest behind her, Sophie had been through a thousand degrees of shock, hysteria and disbelief, and was now beginning to feel very, very angry. Angry with Andre for leaving her on her own; angry with the coroner and the police for being so stupid. Furious with herself for ever believing them when they had insisted that Andre killed himself.

It made no sense. The more she thought about it, the more Sophie realised that it couldn't possibly have been suicide. Why would Andre want to kill himself, just when everything was beginning to come right for them? Why would he choose to poison himself in the bath? And where the hell would he get horse dope from, for goodness' sake? Andre had never even owned a hamster, let alone a racehorse.

She wondered fleetingly if she was deluding herself, unable to accept that Andre would commit the ultimate betrayal. But no; she wasn't that stupid. And if Andre *hadn't* killed himself, that meant that someone else had and they wanted to make it look like suicide.

And that really frightened her.

Today was the day of Andre's funeral, and Sophie had decided that whatever else might happen, she wouldn't let him down. The outfit she wore had been chosen with care. She knew others would be shocked by the glossy black leather, shot through with slashes of scarlet; but she didn't give a damn what others thought. Today, above all days, she would be herself.

Beneath the fitted leather jacket and skirt, she wore nothing but the two diamond-studded nipple rings that Andre had given her, in the days when they had first become lovers. The sensations they gave her with each tiny movement were at once uncomfortable and reassuring. In any case, discomfort was nothing. Pain was the only thing that mattered.

She thought of Marta, for the first time with a certain empathy. Marta had been right about one thing, at any rate. Pain wasn't something to be overwhelmed by; it was something you could use. Bring it to the surface, revel in it, use it . . . and inflict it.

There were more people at the wake than Sophie had expected. A lot more. Who would have imagined that Andre had so many patients? They were all looking at her, staring at her; what they didn't realise was that she was watching them. Wondering which of them might be the murderer.

The choice was an awesome one. Jake Priestley, the black-metal rock star? From what she'd heard, he was perfectly capable of killing someone – but poison? Surely a sharpened crucifix was more his style. Didn't they say that poison was a woman's weapon, wondered Sophie as she shook hands with Lady Anastasia Madeley.

'I'm so sorry . . .' ventured Lady Madeley.

'I'm sure.'

'Andre and I were . . . very close.'

'I don't doubt it.'

Sophie wondered if Anastasia Madeley might have killed Andre. No, that was ridiculous. She might be a high-class slag with the morals of an alleycat, but Anastasia Madeley was no homicidal maniac. And there were so many others here – any one of them might have had a hand in Andre's death. Hal Treves; Peter de Greville; Penny Clivedon . . . any or none of them.

'Sophie?'

She turned and saw Emil Bernhardt, very handsome and just a little creepy with his dark, slicked-back hair and black Italian suit. His handshake was hard, hot, unyielding.

'Emil. I'm glad you could come.'

He did not let go of her gloved hand, but raised it to his lips.

'You look wonderful, Sophie. The most beautiful black widow in the world. Beautiful, captivating, dangerous . . .'

In spite of herself, Sophie gave a dry laugh.

'You talk such shit, Bernhardt.'

A spark of sexual interest passed between them. She could see the hunger in his eyes – the same hunger that had driven Emil and Sophie to that one, reckless fuck in the gymnasium.

'I'd like to fuck you, Sophie.'

'This is a wake, Bernhardt. Are you totally depraved?'

'I know it's what you need. I could make you feel so much better.'

His fingers stroked the side of her face, the black velvet choker at her throat, the generous swell of her breast, guarding its diamond secrets well beneath the tailored leather.

'Sex and death, Sophie. They go together so naturally. Won't you let me show you?'

'Show me, Emil? What is there that you could show me?'

'How to find pleasure in the darkest, the most surprising of circumstances.'

His fingers touched the crest of her pierced nipple, and an electric buzz of need vibrated through her. How could she allow herself to want him so much? Shocked, repelled, excited, she pushed him away.

'No. I've had you once and once is enough.'

'Once is never enough for a woman like you, Sophie.'

'Did you do it, Emil?' she enquired coolly.

Puzzled, he stared back at her.

'Do what?'

'Did you kill Andre?'

'You think I . . .?'

'I don't know what to think', she replied and, turning on her spiky heel, she stalked away.

* * *

Even Davina Templeton had to admit that business at Satin Miss was booming. The books were healthily full, the telephone never seemed to stop ringing, and Mistress Sophie was the most sought-after dominatrix in town.

Sophie's anger and frustration did nothing to diminish her clients' enthusiasm for her very special brand of 'corrective therapy'. On the contrary, they flocked to feel a taste of her discipline, sensing that, as she inflicted pain upon them, her fury was genuine.

One afternoon, Davina came to Sophie's office with a message.

'Are you busy?'

Sophie looked up from a pile of sketches.

'I'm just looking through the new designs. It's so important to keep our range of lingerie innovative and exciting, don't you think?' She pushed one of the sketches across the desk towards Davina. It depicted a tall, leggy brunette wearing the tiniest chastity belt made from pink plastic and gold chains. 'What do you think of this one?'

Reluctantly, Davina looked at it.

'It looks cheap and tarty.'

'My feelings exactly. I thought it might look exceptionally good on you.'

Her blue eyes challenged Davina to retaliate, but Davina knew the price of falling out with Sophie. Like it or not, Laszlo was besotted with Sophie, and wouldn't hear a word against her. And Davina wasn't prepared to risk losing him for the sake of some fleeting victory. She decided to change the subject.

'There's a message for you. A special client has requested a personal visit this afternoon.'

'I'm sure Dee-Dee will make an excellent job of the assignment.'

'No. He specifically requested you. It seems you're getting quite a reputation.'

Sophie's eyes betrayed a flicker of interest.

'Really? He knows about the additional fee?'

'Of course. He's quite happy to pay whatever we ask, in return for absolute discretion.'

'I see. And where am I to attend him?'

'At this address.' Davina handed over a piece of paper. 'It's a flat owned by the Government, near the Houses of Parliament. You'll be seeing Harry Staithes; you know, the right-wing Tory MP.'

So Harry Staithes MP had a craving for pain. Well, Sophie was in the mood to give him exactly what he wanted.

She arrived around two o'clock at the address she had been given, rang the bell and waited. An answerphone buzzed.

'It's Miss Ceretto. Your . . . therapist.'

'Come on up. It's Flat Five, on the second floor.'

She walked through into an ultra-modern lobby, lined with dazzling white marble and filled with semi-tropical plants. Glancing upwards, she saw that the lobby extended upwards, through the building's five storeys, ending in a clear glass roof, many feet above.

The desk was unmanned, so she walked through to the lift, stepped inside and pressed '2'. Moments later she stepped out on to the second floor. The door to Flat Five was immediately opposite and stood slightly ajar.

She entered. It was an ordinary enough flat, nicely decorated but nothing special . . . except for the huge array of correctional instruments displayed on one wall of the sitting room.

In the middle of the sitting-room floor sat Harry Staithes MP – though it was difficult to make any positive identification of him, since he was squatting naked on the carpet, a leather hood completely covering his face and a heavy metal choke-chain hanging from his throat.

A young man in a grey suit glided forward to greet Sophie.

'Miss Ceretto?'

'Yes.'

'Mr Staithes is so glad you could come. He gets extremely tense when his . . . er . . . personal *needs* have not been met for some considerable time.'

'I see. And you are?'

'Godfrey Coulter, Mr Staithes' personal valet. He relies on me to arrange everything for him. Perhaps I should explain a little of what is required?'

'Please do.' Sophie slipped off her coat and handed it to the valet. Underneath, she was wearing her favourite black catsuit with the silver fur trimming, and scarlet ankle boots with intricate lacing and slender heels.

'Mr Staithes has a very demanding job. It requires him to be extremely dominant. The exercise of power . . . shall we say . . . drains him of his vital energies, makes him tense and irritable. He experiences certain urges

134

which cannot easily be satisfied without the assistance of an understanding and discreet partner.'

'I think I understand what you're saying.' Sophie opened her travelling case and took out a pair of fingerless gloves, their palms coated with a thick layer of wire wool. She slipped them on. 'In order to release his tensions, Mr Staithes requires a partner who is able to dominate him and relieve him of the responsibility for his own pleasure?'

'Precisely so. And if I may say so, Mr Staithes is a particular devotee of the whip.'

'Leave him to me. I am sure that I shall be able to accommodate his preferences.'

Godfrey Coulter surveyed the blonde dominatrix with more than a twinge of envy. She was a real looker. Really, it was a pity to waste her on his employer's eclectic sexual tastes. He fantasised briefly about taking her over the polished table in the Cabinet Room.

'I can see that you are a lady of considerable perception.' He gave a small inclination of the head. 'If you will excuse me, I shall leave you to become ... better acquainted.'

The door closed behind him and Sophie was alone with Harry Staithes. Harry Staithes MP. Who'd have thought that a fire-and-brimstone Tory needed to get his kicks from a bitch in a leather catsuit?

She selected a whip from one of those displayed on the wall. It was more than just a whip, it was a real *objet d'art*, a slender whiplash of plaited buckskin intertwined with glittering gold wire. The whip was deceptively short and slender, its fine tip apparently harmless; but Sophie slid it through her fingers with delight, knowing that in its very slenderness and suppleness resided its especially exquisite cruelty.

Staithes crouched motionless on the rug. She knew that he was following her around the room by the sound of her heels on the polished parquet floor, and the twitching of his waking cock confirmed to her that he was filled with delicious anticipation.

The raging tide of anger within her bubbled just below the surface. There was so much fury which she yearned to let out. It was a difficult task to keep it under control.

'You are contemptible,' she whispered, reaching out with the whip and running its tip lightly over the bare flesh of his shoulders and chest. She was rewarded by a faint moan, and saw his nipples strain into erectness.

'You are dirt. You are nothing.' She flicked him, quite softly, and enjoyed the sight of his body tensing with pleasure. 'You are in my power.'

A harder flick this time, just enough to mark him on the sensitive bud of his right nipple.

'You will speak only when you are given permission to do so. And when you do speak, you will call me Mistress. Is that clear?'

Silence.

'You may speak.'

'Yes, Mistress.' Staithes' voice was as thick and sweet as honey and cream.

Sophie walked around him. Tap. Tap. Tap. Her heels measured out the seconds to his ritual humiliation – the humiliation which he craved so desperately.

'Your cock is erect,' she observed. 'You are fantasising. Are you fantasising about me?'

'Yes, Mistress.'

'Worm.' She lashed him quite suddenly and rather hard, just between the shoulder blades.

'Mistress!'

She let fly with the whip again.

'I did not address you. You will make no sound unless I say that you may. Now, worm, you will describe your fantasies to me. In perfect detail. I shall know if you leave anything out.'

She laid the whip across his shoulder.

'Speak, worm.'

His voice was peculiarly hesitant and faint when at last he spoke; a far cry from the front benches in the House, thought Sophie.

'I want you to dominate me, to overpower me, to take me . . .'

'Go on.'

'I have this dream . . . I'm in the House, Black Rod is knocking on the door with his staff. It's huge, thick, bulbous . . . it excites me. And as I look at it, it seems to swell up and get bigger and bigger. I want it inside me, I want it to ram into me and split me in two . . .'

Sophie ran the whip down Staithes' back until it reached the crease between his buttocks. With a quick movement, she pushed the tip into the dark hollow of his anus, twisting it a little so that it tormented the sensitive flesh.

'Mistress – oh, Mistress!' There was a frisson of ecstasy in that voice, and he was working his backside onto the whip, trying to swallow up more and more of it. Quickly she removed it.

'This will not do. I will not have you exciting yourself. Your pleasure is my preserve. Is that clear?'

'Yes, Mistress.'

'Continue. Tell me what you dream of when you masturbate.'

'I dream of the whip. Oh, Mistress, I dream of it cutting into my flesh, making it bleed. It bites me so, it feels like a thousand hornet stings, I can feel the hot blood trickling down over my flesh . . .'

'Enough.'

Sophie walked away from Staithes. She sensed his anticipation, the crackle of his excitement in the air. Good. She would make him wait awhile.

'Mistress?'

'I told you to be silent.' A long pause. 'Stand up.'

He did so, a trifle unsteadily as he had been crouching for so long that the feeling had ebbed out of his legs.

'Spin round.'

'Mistress?'

She raised her voice.

'Do you question my commands?'

'No, Mistress.'

'Then do it.'

He began turning round, rather slowly like an overfed spinning top. He looked ludicrous but Sophie wasn't laughing. She felt only cold, ruthless anger, the anger of everything that had happened to her. If Harry Staithes wanted to suffer, she was not one to disappoint him.

'Faster.'

'I cannot, Mistress, I . . .'

'Faster.' She cracked the whip. 'Faster, do you hear?'

He was spinning crazily now, arms flailing, the chain around his neck clanking as it flew out like a ribbon on a maypole. Sophie watched for a while, then, 'You may stop.'

Staithes tottered to a halt. His breathing was hoarse and rasping as he dragged air into his aching lungs. He swayed on unsteady feet.

'Walk towards me.'

He took a step forward, stumbled and nearly fell. It was obvious that he scarcely knew where he was, let alone which direction to walk in to find his mistress.

'Mistress . . .'

'Do it, disobedient worm!'

He tried again, this time setting off in completely the wrong direction, stumbling, falling to hands and knees on the bare wooden floor. He cut a pathetic figure, a shambling parody of his parliamentary self.

'Mistress, I cannot. I am unworthy.'

'Yes,' she smiled. 'You are, aren't you?'

Towering over him, she raised the whip. There was a superhuman strength in her arm as she brought it down, striking him a sudden cutting blow across the shoulders.

Staithes let out a thin, high wail of pain, but his cock twitched into even greater hardness. The second blow caught him between his buttocks, the tip of the whip snaking through his legs and flicking against the heavy fruits of his testicles. His screams were so loud that the walls of the room seemed to vibrate.

The third blow drew blood, exciting Staithes so dramatically that Sophie feared he might climax and spoil it all. But she was perfectly aware of what she was doing; and as she selected a twelve-inch dildo from the shelf underneath the window, she knew that Harry Staithes was going to get excellent value for money. Why, this could go on for hours and hours.

About a week later, Sophie found herself in the Pink Pearl. She wasn't quite sure why she had come – the business was going perfectly well, there wasn't really anything to discuss with Laszlo. Maybe it was just because she felt comfortable here. Funny that only a couple of years ago when she took a job here as a cocktail waitress, she'd been horrified at the things some of the customers had asked her to do . . .

She poured herself another glass of wine and tried to concentrate on the floor show. Even without Trixie, it was good. With Laszlo's money and Rick's depraved imagination, the Pink Pearl now had one of Europe's sexiest cabarets.

Tonight, the club was staging a special event: its own version of a beauty contest, in which the first prize was a contract to star in a pornographic movie. The stage had been transformed into a mock-up of the film set from *Casablanca*, and a series of girls were giving their all to a very lucky Bogart lookalike.

Rick Strong nudged Sophie's arm.

'Cheer up, kid, it may never happen.'

She flashed him a black look.

'It already did, remember?'

'Yeah. Sorry. It's hard to know what to say.'

Sophie patted Rick's hand.

'No, I'm sorry. I know I'm not exactly easy to live with at the moment.'

'Hardly surprising really. Not since . . .'

'Quite.' Sophie's eyes strayed to the stage. 'So what do you reckon to that one then?'

Rick followed her gaze to the pneumatic blonde whose eager tongue was licking whipped chocolate mousse from Humphrey Bogart's backside.

'All right I suppose. A bit stringy.' He sighed. 'Not a patch on Trixie.'

'She hasn't turned up then?'

'Nope. Dunno why she left like that. Maybe I shouldn't have turned her down for that pay rise. I mean let's face it, for a big-titted bimbo she's amazingly versatile.'

'You miss her?'

'Yeah. Bloody silly, isn't it?'

A hand on her shoulder made Sophie look round. Laszlo was standing over her.

'Piss off, Rick,' he said. 'Sophie and I need to talk.'

He watched Rick's retreating back for a few seconds, then sat down in his seat next to Sophie.

'Drink?'

She shook her head.

'I've got one already, thanks.'

Laszlo ordered up a beer. She watched him out of the corner of her eye. Funny how she'd fought him every inch of the way, resisting his determination to possess her. And now he was the only real constant in her life, and certainly the only person left that she could trust. Laszlo Comaneci would never betray her.

He wouldn't dare.

Laszlo took a sip from his beer.

'I heard ... about Andre. What are you going to do next?'

Her blue eyes seemed to bore right through him.

'I'm going to get even.'

'Even?' Laszlo set down his glass. 'You don't believe it was suicide?'

'Andre was murdered. I'm certain of it.'

To Sophie's surprise, Laszlo replied, 'Yes. I think you may be right.' He tapped his fingers on the table top. 'Look, Sophie, I don't know who's behind all this, but if I can help you I will. For ... old times' sake.' His fingers brushed hers briefly. 'You remember the detective I employed when we were trying to find out what Paolo was up to?'

'Zoë Mellenger?'

'The very same. As a matter of fact I have her on a retainer at the moment, trying to locate Trixie. God knows what's happened to that kid, but I have my suspicions ...' He patted the back of Sophie's hand. 'Zoë's yours if you can use her.'

Much to her own surprise, Sophie didn't hesitate.

'Thanks, Laszlo. You're ... a good friend.'

He smiled. He wanted to kiss her, crush his mouth against hers, but she wouldn't have appreciated the gesture.

'Better than you'll ever know, Sophie.'

He contented himself with a peck on the cheek, drained his beer glass and headed off in search of Rick. Sophie's gaze followed him, but her mind was concentrating on something else.

Revenge.

Somehow, whatever it took, she'd get the man – or the woman – who'd murdered Andre. And when she did, the pain of the bullwhip would be nothing compared to the blistering agony of her vengeance.

Chapter 9

Sophie decided that she had put it off for too long: today was the day when she would have to go through Andre's things.

There was his business to think of, for one thing. All his patients, all those people she'd never met . . . maybe she could keep their treatment going, employ another therapist. But first, she had to make some sense of all the things Andre had left behind.

It felt strange, turning the key in the lock of his consulting room and stepping inside. The meticulous records Andre had kept were all neatly ranged on shelves in a room adjoining the consulting room. She began picking through them, scanning the secrets which Andre had kept locked away.

All in all they were varied enough, bizarre even, but Sophie had seen it all, heard it all . . . and done it all. It took a lot to shock her, and certainly more than a vicar with a fetish for wellington boots, or a fading matinee idol who could only get it up if he took a bath in live mealworms. Was this all that Andre had been hiding from her? Sophie felt almost disappointed.

In a cabinet underneath the shelves were a collection of audio cassettes, labelled with names and dates: 'Clifton Ainsley, 22 April'; 'Jake Priestley, 1 May', 'Reverend John Mortimer, 2 June'.

She selected one at random, picked it up and looked at it. The label read: 'Nanette Duclos, 14 May.' Nanette Duclos? Wasn't she one of the women at Sir Desmond Dukinfield's party? Sophie was sure she'd seen her talking to Andre . . . yes, that was it, she remembered her now. Small, dark, with flashing eyes and a great backside in that tight cocktail dress. Now that Sophie thought about it, she'd seemed . . . edgy. Andre too. She wondered why.

Intrigued, Sophie slid the cassette into the player. So Nanette Duclos was one of Andre's clients. She asked herself what particular hang-up might bug a sexy little Frenchwoman. Walking over to the window, she leaned on the sill and gazed out at the gardens as the tape whirred into life.

Andre's voice cut in first. Sophie could almost imagine he was here in the room: 'You're making excellent progress, Nanette.'

'Thank you, *Docteur*.' Nanette's voice was breathy and soft.

'Now tell me how things have been between you and your husband since we last talked.'

'Better . . . a little better. But Jean-Claude is so very *French*. He believes it is always the man who must make the first move. He used to complain all the time that I was frigid, and now that I am hungry for him, he tells me that I am indecent!'

Sophie yawned. This was very dull. Who'd have thought sex therapy could be so uninteresting? She reached out and almost switched off the tape deck, but something made her stop; something in the tone of Nanette's voice.

'I did it exactly as you said, *Docteur*.'

'Good.'

'I did it exactly as you showed me.' She paused. 'But you see there is a little problem, *Docteur* Andre.' Sophie heard the sound of a passionate, squelchy kiss. 'My husband's penis is simply not as good as yours.'

Sophie wondered why the tape had so unsettled her. It was ridiculous to feel jealousy, just because Andre's sex therapy sessions had gone beyond theory and moved on to the practical. After all, she could hardly complain that he had deceived her when she'd had that brief fling with Emil Bernhardt, and all along she and Laszlo Comaneci had been secretly running an exclusive house of ill-repute.

But it bugged her. No matter how hard she tried to put it out of her mind, the words on the tape just kept on coming back to plague her: 'My husband's penis is not as good as yours, *Docteur* Andre.'

It was probably a thoroughly bad idea, but Sophie decided that she must see this Nanette woman, talk to her face to face. Maybe that way she'd finally get her out of her system. Maybe she'd even hold some clue to the mystery of who had murdered Andre Grafton.

Jumping into her red BMW, Sophie drove out to the southern outskirts of the city. The Duclos house was nice enough, she supposed; a modest Georgian house in a tasteful crescent, on one side of a small park. An ultra-respectable area, hardly the place you'd expect a femme fatale to live. She locked the car and walked up to the front door.

The bell rang for a long time. It seemed to echo through the emptiness. Sophie shifted from one foot to the other, the first chill of doubt making itself felt. There was still time to change her mind and go. What was she going to say?

The door was opened – not by Nanette Duclos but by a hunk in a green and red bathrobe. He had dark eyes, sandy hair, a sensual mouth and a day's growth of stubble on a square jaw. He was gorgeous in a rough sort of way; stockily built but with surprisingly slender, sensitive hands. Sophie breathed in the scent of him. It was luxurious and musky; a mixture of expensive cologne and fresh sex.

He leaned on the doorpost and thrust his hands into the pockets of his robe. It gaped at the neck, offering Sophie an appetising glimpse of a smooth, tanned chest.

'*Oui, Mademoiselle*?'

'I'm sorry to bother you.' Sophie felt oddly tongue-tied. 'You must be Jean-Claude . . .'

His face crinkled into a smile.

'As a matter of fact I am. And you are . . .?'

'Sophie. Sophie Ceretto. I was wondering, could I have a word with Nanette?'

'Ah, you are one of Nanette's friends? I always knew she had charming taste. Please come in.' He stood back

148

and Sophie stepped inside, their bodies brushing briefly. Jean-Claude called up the stairs. '*Chérie? Une amie t'attend.*'

'*Je viens, je viens.*'

'She will be down in a moment. Can I offer you a drink while you wait?'

'That would be lovely.'

Jean-Claude ushered Sophie into a sitting room, expensively decorated with Regency furniture, gilded mirrors and an ostentatious chandelier which threatened to decaptitate anyone over six feet tall.

'Crème de cassis? With a little crushed ice?'

'Thank you.'

Jean-Claude poured Sophie's drink and sat down beside her on the antique day-bed. She couldn't help noticing how close he was, their bodies almost but not quite touching; and the words on the tape reverberated in her head: 'My husband's penis is not as good as yours, *Docteur* Andre.' And here Jean-Claude was, playing the great Gallic seducer. She almost smiled as she wondered how he would react if he realised that she knew all about his sexual shortcomings.

'You have known Nanette long?'

'Not really. But I feel I know her very well.' *Better than she realises*, thought Sophie. *And better than you . . .*

Jean-Claude stretched out his muscular legs. His robe fell open at the thigh but he seemed not to care in the least that Sophie could glimpse the ripe fruits of his testicles, or the tip of his flaccid penis. *If this is the preferred French method of seduction*, Sophie thought, *you can keep it.*

149

'Strange she hasn't mentioned you,' remarked Jean-Claude. 'Or perhaps she wishes to keep you to herself, for fear I will take . . . an interest in you.'

'Perhaps.' Sophie was beginning to find Jean-Claude less than appealing. At first he had seemed just a good-looking hunk, muscle-bound and testosterone-packed. Now he was beginning to be more predatory than attentive. If Nanette really was the scheming little tart she thought she was, then she and Jean-Claude deserved each other. 'But I'm sure she has nothing at all to worry about.'

She shifted her position on the day-bed slightly, but Jean-Claude moved too, sliding even closer so that his thigh lay along hers, the heat of his sweaty, over-perfumed, sex-reeking body inescapable through the thin crepe of her summer trousers.

'Between you and me,' said Jean-Claude confidentially, 'Nanette is a very jealous woman.'

'Really? And does she have anything to be jealous about?'

'That depends,' replied Jean-Claude, lowering his voice to a conspiratorial whisper, 'on whether or not you accept my dinner invitation. I know the most wonderfully discreet little bistro in the West End . . .'

Sophie glanced down. She could hardly fail to notice that Jean-Claude's dick was thrusting its way through the gaping front of his bathrobe. It was short, thin and looked in danger of deflating at any moment. So *that* was why Nanette preferred Andre . . .

She met Jean-Claude's gaze.

'You're asking me out to dinner?'

'*Absolument*. I love to have dinner with beautiful women.'

'And afterwards?'

His fingers brushed the back of her hand.

'A little champagne, a little . . .'

'A little *dick*? Sorry, Jean-Claude, I only screw men, not underdeveloped schoolboys.' She glanced towards a figure standing aghast in the doorway. 'Oh Nanette, *darling*, how lovely to see you again. Jean-Claude was just showing me his penis. It isn't very impressive is it? No wonder you needed Andre to show you how to have fun.' She looked from Nanette to Jean-Claude and back again. 'I think we should talk alone, don't you? There are some things you might find . . . embarrassing.'

Nanette and Jean-Claude exchanged looks.

'*Vas-y*. Get out, Jean-Claude. We'll talk about this later.'

Jean-Claude left the room without even saying goodbye to Sophie. The door closed softly behind him and Sophie heard his footsteps fading into the distance.

'Good,' she said. 'Now we can talk.'

Nanette flicked the tip of her tongue nervously across her parched lips.

'You're Sophie, aren't you? Sophie Ceretto.'

'Bravo.'

'Why are you here?'

'To talk about you. You and Andre. Had a lot of fun together, didn't you?'

'I . . .'

'Please, Nanette, don't insult my intelligence by telling me that nothing went on in that consulting room.' Sophie reached into the pocket of her jacket and took out a copy of the cassette tape. 'I've heard it all, every sordid word of it.'

Nanette's face fell.

'*Non*, Sophie, you must believe me, it was not like that!'

'Like what?'

'It was not ... how you say? ... an affair. It was ...' Suddenly, and to Sophie's acute embarrassment, Nanette broke down in floods of tears. Through her sobs, she tried haltingly to explain what had happened. '*Docteur* Andre, he was a saint! He helped me so much, he taught me how to be a woman ...'

Sophie sighed.

'You're telling me all of this was part of your *treatment*?'

Nanette nodded vigorously.

'*Mais oui, exactement!* I was frigid, I did not know how to respond to my husband, I could not feel pleasure. And *Docteur* Andre, he showed me how to make my husband feel pleasure also ... Can you imagine how I felt when he died? Can you, Sophie? He was the one who saved me, and he helped so many, not just me!'

In spite of herself, Sophie found herself consoling Nanette, slipping an arm about her shoulders and offering her a tissue to dry her tears. She'd been wrong about the Frenchwoman, that much was obvious. The girl might have hero-worshipped Andre, but she was no homicidal maniac. She thought of Nanette's words: 'He helped so many,' and her heart sank. If the killer really was one of

Andre's patients, it was going to take more than a little luck to find out which one.

Zoë Mellenger drew up a chair and nodded to Stephanie Lace.

'Take a seat.'

Stephanie sat, but looked ill at ease, searching Sophie and Zoë's faces for answers. She fiddled with the end of her Liberty print scarf.

'What's all this about?'

'Zoë's a detective, she just needs to ask you a few questions, that's all.' Sophie perched on the edge of the reception desk. Her metallic blue fingernails flashed barely inches from Stephanie's face. 'About what happened to Andre.'

'But I've already been over it all with the police. And I don't know anything!'

'Let me be the judge of that.' Zoë towered over Stephanie. 'You want to help, don't you?'

'Yes, of course, but . . .'

Zoë put up her hand.

'Let's start with Andre's patients. You knew them all, of course?'

Stephanie shrugged.

'By sight. Some of them to talk to a little.' She looked uncomfortable. 'You have to understand, most of them didn't want to be here any longer than they had to.'

'They were worried about being seen here?'

'Wouldn't you be, if you were a TV star or a famous agony aunt? They only came here because they were desperate for help and knew we would be completely discreet about their . . . problems.'

'Ah yes, their *problems*.' Zoë consulted her notebook. 'The Black Count – you remember him?'

'It'd be hard to forget him. Only that isn't his real name, he's called Jake Priestley.'

'Tell me about him.'

'He's the lead singer in one of those cult black-metal bands. Funny really, he's quite ordinary and polite when you get talking to him. Bit of a pussycat really. Pays his bills on time, too.'

'And his sexual problems? You were aware of them?'

'Something about sado-masochism, I think. He was worried he couldn't get turned on if he wasn't thinking about pain. And I think he was fed up with the life he was leading, you know, wanted to get out of the business but he didn't know how.'

'And can you think of any reason why Mr Priestley might have a grudge against Doctor Grafton?'

'Hardly. I mean, Andre was helping him to get his life back. Why would he want to kill him?'

'Why indeed.' Zoë ticked the name off the list. Black-mail? Maybe. These murder cases usually came down to sex, and once sex was involved you could bet that there was someone trying to make money out of someone else's secrets. 'How about Lady Anastasia Madeley?'

Stephanie pulled a face.

'Don't care much for her.'

'Why not?'

'She's . . . can I say what I think?'

'There's not much point in any of us being here if you don't,' cut in Sophie.

'She's a cow. Thinks she can have any man she wants.'

And can she? wondered Sophie. Out loud, she commented: 'Anastasia Madeley has made a fortune out of divorcing wealthy husbands. I'd have thought she was quite capable of killing Andre.'

'Possibly,' agreed Zoë. 'But why would she *want* to?'

They worked their way slowly through the long list of Andre's more bizarre and temperamental clients: Hal Treves, Saskia Clifton, Nanette Duclos and all the rest. Zoë walked across to the window and opened it. Taking in a few breaths of fresh air, she turned round.

'That's all of them, Stephanie?'

'All that I can think of.'

'There must be something else,' protested Sophie.

Stephanie got up from her chair, walked into Andre's office and started rummaging in his desk drawers.

'What are you doing?' asked Zoë, puzzled.

Stephanie closed the last of the drawers and stood up.

'It's not here.'

'What isn't?'

'The card. It was delivered to Andre by hand, the day before he was ... the day before he died.'

'What was on it?' demanded Sophie.

'He didn't want me to see, but I sneaked a look. It had a pink heart like this ...' She drew on her notepad. 'Oh, and some writing ... a date, time and place I think. Market Square, that was the place, I can't remember the rest.'

'Anything else you can remember about it? Did you recognise the handwriting?'

Stephanie shook her head.

'It was typed.'

'OK.' Zoë let the tension flood out of her in a long, slow sigh. 'Look, I'll be in touch if I need to ask you any more questions. And keep this to yourself, yeah?'

'Yes. OK. Can I go now?'

'Sure you can.'

When Stephanie had gone, Zoë and Sophie faced each other across Andre's desk.

'Do you think she knows something she's not telling us? I mean, she seems uncomfortable about being questioned.'

Zoë shook her head.

'I doubt it. She's probably scared stiff we'll notice that she's fiddled twenty quid from the petty cash. No, I think she's told us everything she knows about Andre and his patients. I just wish I had that card.'

'You think it could have been from whoever killed him?'

'Who knows? Bit of a coincidence though, coming the day before he died.'

'You'll look into it?'

'Of course – that's what I'm being paid for. And in the meantime . . .'

'Mmm?'

'Perhaps you could follow up some of Andre's clients? You know, get a feel for whether or not they might be involved.'

'Don't worry.' Sophie stretched out her long, slim legs. 'I'll give it my *very* personal touch. One way or another, we're going to find out who killed Andre – and why.'

The next afternoon, Sophie went to the bathing pond for a swim.

She loved swimming; it cleared her head. While you were swimming, you had to concentrate on what you were doing. You couldn't dwell on the things that wouldn't let you go. She could have done a few lengths of the private pool at the Hall, but she craved company and fresh air.

The bathing pond was discreet, exclusive – and mixed. Discerning swimmers of both sexes came here to bathe nude in a natural lake screened by trees. At its centre lay a small grassy island, presently adorned with the bodies of naked sunbathers.

It was a tranquil place, and Sophie let the hot sunshine caress her body as she cut her way through the bracingly cold water. It felt good to be naked, floating free of the cares which dragged her down.

There were few swimmers in the pool at this time of day, so she was surprised when a young man drew level with her in the water, measuring his pace to hers.

She rolled onto her back, swam backstroke for a while, then flipped back onto her belly. He was still there, swimming alongside. She stole a look at him. He wasn't bad-looking, not bad at all. Wet golden hair was slicked back from a high-cheekboned face in which blue eyes glittered. Droplets of water trickled and splashed over powerful shoulders as he drove his way across the lake.

He smiled. On some mad impulse she smiled back, then kicked hard and left him behind. Head down, scything through the water, she did not hear him moving up behind her; had no idea that he was still with her until she felt his hands slipping around her, cupping her breasts, lightly stroking the hardness of her nipples.

She thrashed in the water, pushing him away.

'Now hang on, what do you think you're . . .?'

But he merely laughed, and drew her back to him, this time belly to belly. And this time she did not struggle. She felt hungry, and here was someone who might have the power to assuage that hunger. A sexy stranger, someone she would probably never even see again. Maybe it was better that way.

Treading water, they kissed. The stranger's hands roamed Sophie's body, sliding easily over her flesh in the water.

Her look was questioning: 'Here?'

His smile was her reply, and she felt his thigh easing its way between hers, rubbing flesh on flesh, the hardness of bone and muscle teasing reluctant pleasure from the opening petals of her secret flower. It felt good, wickedly good, and yet . . .

'No, not here.' She shook her head. Taking his hand, she swam towards the island, making for the wooded side where few people ever bothered to go. 'Here is so much better.'

They slid out of the water on to hot, dry grass. Sophie's head was spinning, her body cold yet burning inside. Was she really doing this? Was she really lying naked on a

158

grassy bank with a complete stranger, letting him kneel between her thighs, pressing his lips against the lips of her sex, pushing his tongue into the slippery-wet heart of her womanhood?

She knew that it must be true as pleasure pierced her with steel-hard precision. Whoever this guy was, he knew exactly what he was doing. His tongue was velvet-smooth on the fragile petals of her inner labia; and she tilted her hips in instinctive response as he traced slow, concentric circles towards the yearning, sap-filled stigma of her clitoris. It offered itself to him, straining as it pushed its way from beneath the fleshy hood which encircled it; yet still he did not touch it.

'Ah. Ah yes . . .'

She breathed out her pleasure in slow, soft gasps as her unknown lover's hands slipped between her thighs and his fingertip slid into the waiting haven of her sex.

'Oh please – don't stop.'

It seemed he had no intention of doing any such thing. At last he took Sophie's clitoris between his lips and began to suck on it, at the very same time flicking his tongue-tip across its head.

'Take me, take me, take me,' she moaned. It seemed like a dream, and the faraway voice sounded like someone else's; but the pleasure was very definitely hers.

He took her to the very edge of climax and held her there, making her twist and turn on the grass as she tried vainly to bring herself off. His skill was too great and in exhaustion she fell back, breathless with effort and throbbing with unsatisfied passion.

Without a word he got off her and rolled her on to her belly, so that her cheek lay against the sun-warmed grass. His fingers scratched lightly down her back, clawed playfully at her buttocks, and she lifted her bottom, pushing herself in his face. *Take me, take me, take me.*

He took her as soundlessly as he had licked her out, the cool sabre of his prick tunnelling deep into her hot belly. This time she cried out, a long, aching moan of joy as he filled her up and possessed her. And then the frenzy began.

Their fucking was wild but almost silent, their bodies moving frantically together, heedless of anyone who might happen upon them. But the only sound was the soft rhythm of their breathing, quickening as pleasure deepened and the moment of crisis approached.

Sophie could feel her orgasm overwhelming her, engulfing her in a secret warmth which no one else could share. Slippery wetness dripped from her pussy, soaking her thighs; her nipples tingled and ached; her clitoris burned with desperate anticipation. Her unknown lover's nails raked down her back but she cared nothing for the discomfort; if anything, it stimulated her to even greater excitement.

At last it happened. She shuddered, her body stiffening into complete rigidity for a few ecstatic moments, then sinking down into a warm and wonderful afterglow.

Her lover ejaculated with cold efficiency, climbed off her and stood up. When Sophie opened her eyes, she was vaguely surprised to find that he was gone.

It wasn't until later, when she had swum back to the

shore and taken herself into the changing rooms for a shower, that Sophie began to wonder if something might be wrong.

Her back stung a little. Well it would, wouldn't it? Her chance encounter had been enthusiastic to say the least, and her one-time lover had raked passionate claws over her flesh. Sophie found a mirror and, standing with her back towards it, let her towel fall, craning her head to see the damage.

Her heart missed a beat, then began thumping wildly. Amid the mass of scratches and welts, two words had been crudely scrawled across her back in scarlet lipstick or paint. They read:

'YOU NEXT'.

Chapter 10

Hal Treves was feeling good. Very good. All in all, life couldn't be better.

His problems were all behind him. In fact, he wondered why he had worried about them so much. That business with Dr Grafton had been a bit of a shocker, but that was all forgotten now. He whistled softly to himself as he slipped on his jacket and pushed open the door to the lecture theatre. Inside was the usual noisy jumble of gossiping, laughing students. Generally he envied them their freedom, their irresponsibility, their biological optimism. But today he didn't envy anybody anything. The urges were gone. He was free! Today he felt great.

'OK everyone, let's . . . oh . . .'

His words tailed off as he caught sight of the blonde woman in the front row. She was . . . breathtaking. What was more, he hadn't seen her before.

He pushed a handful of photocopied sheets at a youth in a 'Sid the Sexist' T-shirt.

'Hand these out would you? Two sheets each.'

Hal turned his attention to the unknown blonde. She was hardly your typical student – she was much too classy for that; classy but with just a hint of the high-class tart.

His gaze travelled up from high-heeled ankle boots and seamed stockings to a very nice black leather miniskirt, clinging white bodysuit and flawless scarlet nails. The backside under that miniskirt was rounded but firm, just begging to be spanked. The woman's oval face was dominated by cornflower-blue eyes and framed by golden blonde hair, pulled back into a high ponytail.

Glossy red lips smiled encouragingly at him. He took it as an invitation.

'Hi. I'm Hal Treves.'

'Yes.' That same smile again. The smile which just *might* mean it was his lucky day. 'So I heard.'

'And you're . . .?'

'Sophie.'

'Have I seen you at my lectures before?'

'I shouldn't think so. I've only just joined the course.'

'And you're enjoying it so far?'

The blue eyes lingered. They felt like a caress on his skin.

'It just got better.'

Hal couldn't take his eyes off the girl all through his lecture. He was pretty sure his lecturing technique suffered, but no one seemed to notice. That was the thing about students . . . but not this one. Not the mysterious and delectable Sophie. Sophie with the smackable backside.

He ran his finger along the inside of his collar. His throat felt constricted and dry. No, no. He mustn't give in to these wild impulses, the way he'd given in to them before. Why had he bothered going through all that humiliating therapy with Doctor Grafton, if not to learn how to resist?

It was no use. She was crossing her legs now, too slowly for decency, letting him catch a glimpse of what she was hiding underneath that so-short skirt. As she moved, he noticed how smooth and firm her thighs were, how teasingly full her breasts underneath her white bodysuit. A girl like that oughtn't to be let out without a government health warning. He made up his mind that after the lecture he would turn right round and head back to the Senior Common Room, not giving Sophie a second thought.

Thirty seconds after the end of the lecture, he was talking to her.

'How did you enjoy the lecture?'

'There were one or two points I didn't quite grasp.'

'That's a pity. Is there anything I can explain?'

Sophie's lips curved into a smile. The very tip of her tongue moistened her glossy mouth.

'I was wondering if you'd be willing to give me . . . a private tutorial. I'm a very indisciplined student, I'm afraid. I need firm handling, if you know what I mean.'

Hal felt an unseen hand sliding down his belly to the root of his stiffening prick; cool, invisible fingers curling about the hot flesh and stroking it into life.

'I . . .' *Say no*, said the sensible voice in his head. *Refuse, she can only bring you trouble.* 'I'd be delighted,' he replied. 'Why don't you come back to my room right now?'

There was no doubt about it, thought Hal as they walked back towards his office. Sophie was a real looker – and there was more to it than that. She had an indefinable charisma, a sexual allure which turned heads along every corridor they walked down.

Sex burned between his thighs, a delicious heaviness in his balls telling him that he had to have this one, even if he never had another woman. This one was special. This one could make him come in his pants, just with one touch of her silken fingers. And if he was to run his hand over that smooth backside . . .

Opening the door, he ushered her inside. He couldn't help noticing that she was braless underneath that stretchy white thing. Braless and mobile, the pink tips of her nipples straining against the fabric. Nice. Very nice.

Sophie pushed the door shut and leaned her back against it.

'I want you to fuck me,' she said with perfect simplicity.

Hal felt hot and cold. There was a telltale stickiness in his pants, where his cock had leaked lubricating fluid into the silk of his boxer shorts.

'You want me . . .?'

'. . . to give me a good fucking. Yes. Don't you want to, Hal?'

'Of course I do, only . . .'

'Don't disappoint me, Hal.' She walked up to him and put her arms about his neck. 'Please. Afterwards you can spank me if you like.'

He could hardly turn her away, could he? She was begging for it, and her hot, sweet young body was pressed up against him, her breasts squashed against his chest, her hips softly grinding against the painful hardness of his cock.

He kissed her, and suddenly all his animal instincts took over. It was as though someone had thrown a lever and switched off all his inhibitions.

'If that's what you want, darling . . .'

Hal's strong hands tore off the leather jacket and greedily possessed Sophie's willing body. She was hard and muscular underneath the superficial softness of her smooth skin. Their mouths met again and again, tongues hungrily jousting, thrusting, exploring.

'How the hell do I get into this?' he grunted.

Sophie answered him by taking his hands and sliding them down her thighs to the hem of her skirt.

'Push it up,' she whispered. 'Go on.'

He did as he was bidden. Stockings and suspenders. Suspenders! Oh but he loved a woman in stockings and a lacy suspender belt. It was almost as if this girl had found out about all his sexual preferences and turned herself into the woman of his dreams. But that, of course, was a ludicrous idea.

Pushing up the leather mini, he discovered that his progress was halted by the bodysuit.

'How . . .?'

'Unfasten the poppers. They just snap open, it's easy.'

Her hand guided his, and he quickly unfastened the pop-fasteners. The moist gusset sprang back to reveal plump, shaven pussy-lips and an ocean of divine wetness.

It was all too much. He had to have her right now.

Sliding his hands under her backside, Hal hoisted Sophie up and pushed her across his desk. She sprawled there so invitingly, her thighs outspread and her pretty quim indecently close, that it was all he could do to keep himself from spurting all over her.

His fingers clawed down the top of her bodysuit, exposing rosy, kissable breasts. Squeezing and biting them, he unzipped his cock.

'You darling bitch,' he breathed. And he entered her in a single stroke, shivering with delight at the ease of it. She was amply lubricated, the tight sheath of her womanhood beautifully greased with the fruits of her own desire.

Oh yes. So very, very easy. She moved like a dream beneath him, her hips rising and falling to meet his thrusts. He was so sensitive, so hyped-up that he had to bite his tongue to keep from coming too quickly.

'Bitch, bitch, bitch,' he gasped as he drove into her. Her fingers raked his back through his shirt, her voice a husky whisper of pure sex.

'Do it to me, Hal. Do it to me. Take me, have me, shoot your spunk right up inside . . .'

And he would have done precisely that, in the next few seconds, if it hadn't been for Sophie. Anticipating the moment with uncanny precision, she pushed him off her.

'What . . .?'

She was surprisingly strong, thought Hal in the lightning-flash between fucking her and being pinned to the desk by her smooth, moist thighs. So strong, in fact, that he couldn't move an inch. Or was it that he didn't want to? He stared up at her as she straddled him; not quite sure what to think as the sharp edge of the desk cut into his backside. It was weird, humiliating even; but on the other hand her thighs were warm and moist, and he was achingly close to orgasm.

'Sophie – what are you *doing*?'

Her response was to reach down and grab him by the balls.

'I'm doing . . . *this*.'

She squeezed – hard – and he let out a cry of pain.

'Oh God no! Sophie, you little bitch!'

She did it again, and he squirmed under the relentless power of her cruel caress. His head swam. Pain; pleasure. The two were so very close that it was easy to be confused about what he was really feeling. Funny that he'd never realised it before.

'Tell me, Hal.'

'Tell you . . . what?'

'About Andre.'

'Andre Grafton?'

'You know what I'm talking about.'

Sophie's thighs were caressingly tight about his, and as she relaxed her grip on his testicles, Hal almost thought he might come. He was so very close to the blessed release of pleasure.

'I only wish I did.'

Her hand tightened its grip a fraction.

'Tell me what you know about Andre Grafton's death.'

'It was . . . it was suicide, that's all I know. Took an overdose of something, didn't he?'

'Don't fuck me about, Hal.'

169

This time she really did squeeze hard, and her sharpened fingernails dug into the soft flesh of his seed-sac.

'Aah!'

'Tell me, Hal, or it gets worse.'

'Stop, stop that!'

And still another fraction tighter.

'Well?'

'Look, I'll tell you anything you want to know. Anything, do you understand?'

'Good.'

This time she relaxed her grip completely, but left her
fingers lightly cupping Hal's balls. She didn't want him
getting any funny ideas; a little reminder of his vulnerability would do him no end of good.

'I'm waiting, Hal.'

'What is it I'm supposed to know?'

'Grafton. Tell me everything you know about him.'

'He was a doctor. A sex-doctor, very discreet. I went to
see him about a problem . . .'

'Yes. I know about your little weakness, Hal. Don't you
think you ought to show a little self-restraint? Spanking
and screwing your students can get you into a lot of
trouble.'

'He was giving me therapy. It was going well. Then all
of a sudden, I hear that he's dead. Killed himself.'

'You went to the funeral?'

'No. No, I didn't want to be spotted. I sent a wreath.
Look, I just want to forget about it, OK? I don't know
who you are or what I'm supposed to have done . . .'

Sophie looked down at him. He had honesty written all

170

over his face. Honesty and weakness. She'd seen that expression on a hundred clients at Satin Miss. Like Hal Treves, they were weak men who cared for little but finding some safe way to indulge their weaknesses. Disappointment stabbed at her and she took it out on Hal, giving his balls a final and savage squeeze.

It was too much for him. With an almost silent scream, he climaxed, his semen fountaining out in hot spurts all over the front of his shirt.

Climbing off him, Sophie wiped her hand on Hal's trousers.

'Thank you,' she said. 'You've been very . . . helpful.'

He sat up, his eyes following her like a lost dog's as she buttoned up her bodysuit, smoothed down her skirt and walked towards the door.

'Sophie,' he whispered.

She turned and looked at him.

'What?'

'Please don't go. Not yet. Please . . . stay and do it to me again.'

The next name on Sophie's list was Jake Priestley.

It wasn't difficult for a hot Goth chick to get a backstage pass, as Sophie quickly discovered when she arrived at the gig dressed like Siouxsie Sioux's sluttish sister.

Necrophilia were playing one of their 'smaller' venues, a thousand-seater on the outskirts of London. Not that there were any seats as such – they had all been ripped out – and the place was swarming with kids in black leather and heavy silver jewellery.

There was some competition, it was true, but the girls here were amateurs. Middle-class kids with black lipstick and ripped fishnet tights, wetting their M & S knickers for a glimpse of the Black Count himself.

After the gig, Sophie showed her backstage pass and pushed her way through the crowd of screaming girls. The after-show party was in full swing and already one or two of them had been given the nod and palmed off on roadies.

'Cool chick,' observed the band's drummer, swigging from a bottle of ice-cold Bud. He gave Sophie's backside a grope. 'Bet you give great blow-jobs. Ever had sex with a big star?'

She turned and gave him a contemptuous look.

'Why? Have you?'

The Black Count was nowhere to be seen, so Sophie forced her way through the crowd to the road manager.

'I want to see the Count.'

He looked her up and down.

'They all do, darlin'. Course, I could get you in to see him if I wanted. If you were . . . let's say . . . really nice to me.'

Sophie sighed inwardly. Was she really going to have to screw this unappealing, overweight, balding prat to get to where she wanted to be? She knew his type: all talk.

'So you can get me into the Count's dressing room?'

'Maybe. Let's just say you need to pass a little audition first, shall we?' He unzipped his jeans and took out a flabby cock, gave it a few wanks and presented it to Sophie as though it were some kind of trophy. 'Do a good job on this, darlin', who knows who you'll get to screw before the night's over.'

At that moment, a tall man in a suit grabbed the road manager by the shoulder. He looked out of place to say the least in this black mass of a party.

'Put it away, Pete. She's too good for you.'

'Now hang on, Tarq . . .'

'I've got you a couple of nice Japanese girls, they're waiting for you in the trailer. Now piss off, and don't say I never do anything for you.'

Pete zipped himself up and departed with several backward glances. The man in the suit folded his arms and surveyed Sophie.

'Nice. Very nice. I especially like the tits. Implants are they? Now listen, I know somebody who'd really like to meet you.'

'Oh really?'

'Really. Big fan of the Count are you?'

'You could say.'

'Pretty cool for a groupie, aren't you?' Tarq nodded his approval. 'Look, I'm Tarq Foley, the Count's agent. He's been feeling a bit down lately, he needs a bit of . . . cheering up, a kind of special treat, get my drift?'

'I think so.'

'Good. Because I'm counting on you to do the biz.'

Tarq led her through a door and down a narrow, dingy passageway which smelt of alcohol, sweat and illegal substances. Black candles burned in wrought-iron candlesticks outside the last door on the right.

'Go in, kid. Make sure he rises to the occasion.'

Sophie's heart thumped as she turned the door handle. What was Jake Priestley really like? Was he just some kid in black leather trousers, or did he live up to the publicity hype – a satanic messiah with a taste for kinky sex? It looked as if she was about to find out.

Rock music blared out of the dressing room as Sophie opened the door and stepped inside. The Count was standing with a glass in his hand, his black and white make-up slightly smeared by heat and sweat, giving him an even more menacing appearance than usual. He was taller than Sophie remembered him, thin and wiry in his black leather stage costume with studded gauntlets and narrow-toed boots.

'Your agent says I'm to cheer you up,' ventured Sophie. The Count looked back at her, drained his glass and threw it at the wall. It smashed in a mess of splintered glass, releasing a stench of spilt whisky.

'My agent can go to hell.' He passed the back of his gloved hand across his mouth. 'What do you want?'

'You.'

Sophie stepped forward and switched off the CD player. The silence which followed was perfect and unnerving.

The Count shook his head, waved her aside.

'I'm not interested, OK? Not tonight.'

Sophie ran her black fingernails down the smooth leather of his stage costume, brushing the generous outline of his swollen cock.

'You look interested. You *feel* interested.'

Her fingers squeezed him gently. He let out a low gasp, but pushed her away.

'I told you, no.'

He turned away, but Sophie pursued him, speaking to his back.

'Why not? You're not afraid are you?'

He laughed. But the laughter was not quite convincing.

'Why should I be afraid?'

He looked round at her.

'Look, let me spell it out. I'm sick of crazy women who want me to beat them up and rape them. I'm sick of virgins begging me to deflower them. I'm sick of it all . . .'

Sophie slid her hand round his waist and smoothed it down, slowly but deliberately, to the ripe stalk of his penis.

'Not every woman wants that,' she purred. 'Some women want something very different.'

'What do you mean?'

'Some women understand what you really want. They want to bring *you* pain.'

Silence.

'That's what you want, isn't it?'

The Count did not answer, but she felt him tremble as she unzipped his flies and thrust her hand inside. He was naked underneath the close-fitting leather, the shaft of his cock ending in a fat, bulbous dome which oozed moisture.

'I know you want it. I know you want me. Just leave everything to me, OK?'

He offered himself to her with an immense excitement, a lust underpinned by grateful relief. For too long he had been cast as the monster, forced to play a part he'd grown tired of years ago.

'What are you going to do to me?' he asked her, his voice breathless and soft as a child's.

'I'm going to fuck you. I'm going to strip you, and bind you and gag you so you can't cry out. I'm going to make you feel pain like you've never felt before.'

His cock stiffened in her hand.

'I'm going to do to you what you've done to all those girls. I'm going to show you how good it feels . . .'

She stripped him, clawing the leather from his body. The ripe scent of his sweat-soaked flesh excited her, made her throb between her legs, made her hungry for him even though that wasn't why she was here. She had to keep reminding herself of who – and what – the Black Count might turn out to be.

Wrenching down his leather shirt, she bared him to the waist and made him sit down. She used his belt to bind his wrists to the chair back, then took a length of cord from the pile of stage props and tied his ankles securely to the legs.

'Now you're mine,' she told him.

'Yours,' he echoed, half hypnotised by this blonde nemesis in a tight black miniskirt and see-through black lace bra.

'Mine to do with exactly as I wish. What *shall* I do, I wonder?'

'Please, please . . .'

She had brought a small bag with her. She reached into it and took out a black chiffon scarf.

Lifting her skirt, she revealed the naked beauty of her shaven pussy, framed by the lacy tops of her black hold-up stockings. Passing the chiffon scarf between her thighs, she moistened it with her juices, impregnating it with the musky scent of her sex. The Count groaned, his eyes wide with longing.

'You talk too much,' she told him. 'You really must learn to take your pleasure in silence. It's the ultimate discipline, you know.'

She bound his face tightly with the scarf, passing it round his nose and mouth several times before tying it at the back.

'There,' she smiled. 'Breathe in the scent, let it fill you. It is the scent of your mistress.'

It was surprising how many treasures you could pack into a small travelling bag. Sophie took out silver clamps, a golden leopard's paw with wickedly sharp claws, a riding crop with a handle in the shape of a naked girl.

'Now, how shall we begin your punishment?' Sophie let the Count squirm for a while in a silent agony of frustration as she feigned indecision. 'The crop? No, I don't think you're quite ready for it? The claw? Ah, but I want to save the best for last.'

She picked up the clamps. They were fashioned in the shape of dragons' heads, one with eyes of garnet, the other set with peridots.

'Lovely, aren't they?' She held them inches from the Count's face, turning them over and over in her hand. 'See the jaws? The teeth are very sharp. Wouldn't you like to feel them?'

She held them open for a moment, the dragons' eyes sparkling in the light from the single fly-specked bulb, dangling on its gently-swaying flex. The Count's eyes were wide, his gaze a fixed stare. He couldn't take his eyes off the clamps, anticipating the pain, anticipating the pleasure too . . .

'What's that? You would? I'm so glad.'

Bending over the Count, she applied the clamps to his bare nipples, releasing them simultaneously so that the jaws snapped shut on the flesh. The Count's scream was audible even through the black chiffon gag which filled his mouth. Sophie smiled and shook her head.

'What's that you said? The pain is not quite enough for you? Well I don't want to disappoint you.'

She noticed that the Count's cock was impressively erect, performing its own jerky dance as pleasure, pain; pain, pleasure alternated, stabbing electrical shocks through his body. Really and truly, he was an excellent pupil. Sophie wondered why Andre hadn't tried this innovative form of therapy on his patient.

She took up the riding crop and slapped it a couple of times across her palm. It made a satisfying sound; the sound of discipline.

'Ready? Of course you are. Your dear little penis is straining fit to burst. But you won't come, will you? I should have to punish you if you came all over your lovely leather trousers. You mustn't come before your mistress gives you permission.'

She struck him lightly across the tight arc of his penis. He squirmed, writhed, his body tense and sweating. A fine trickle of sweat ran down between the tit-clamps.

'Not hard enough? I'm so sorry. Let me remedy that.'

With the second swipe of the riding crop Sophie began beating him in earnest. Unpredictability was one of the hallmarks of a really sensual beating. She had discovered that in her long apprenticeship in domination. Never let your slave anticipate correctly where the next blow will come. Just when he is certain that you will beat him again across the back or the thighs, direct the tip of the whip between his legs, or strike him across his yearning, slavering mouth.

She worked him into a frenzy of need, his cock almost bursting with desire, clear sex-fluid oozing from its swollen tip. She thirsted for the taste of that salty, juicy plum, but pleasure would be for later. For now she must have the truth.

Tearing the gag from his lips, she took up the leopard's claw and dragged it down over his chest. He gasped, drawing air into his tormented lungs in hoarse, halting breaths.

'Are you ready now? Ready to tell me the truth?'

The Count's eyes registered incomprehension.

'The truth?'

A flick of the crop, precisely directed at the right dragon's-head clamp, provoked a groan of delicious pain.

'Don't play games with me, Jake. I want the truth about Andre Grafton. You killed him, didn't you?'

The Count stared back at her.

'*Killed* him? I was right first time. You really are crazy.'

Swipe. Swipe. Swipe.

'Don't fuck me about. Why did you kill Andre? Is that how you get your kicks?'

'Lady, you gotta believe me, I don't know what you're talking about.'

Taking hold of the tit-clamps, Sophie gave them a savage clockwise twist.

'I don't have to believe you, Jake. I don't have to believe a word you say if I choose not to. Now tell me the truth or it gets much, much worse.'

Was that hope she detected in his grey eyes? Was he holding back on her precisely so that she would make him suffer even greater torments? She let go of him and stood back.

'No. Correction. Tell me everything you know about Andre Grafton's death, or I shall simply leave you like this.'

'You can't!' blurted the Count. 'I can't bear it, you have to help me.'

Sophie folded her arms.

'I'm waiting.'

The Count licked his lips nervously.

'Andre Grafton was my therapist. He was helping me with a few . . . problems.'

'Sexual problems?'

'I . . . yeah.'

'I know all about your problems, Jake. I know what you like to do to your lovers. I'm here to show you how it feels . . . and to find out the truth.'

'I heard he was dead about three days after it happened.'

'Why so long afterwards?'

Jake shrugged.

'I was playing Norway. London gossip doesn't travel *that* fast. If it hadn't been for the Internet . . .'

'Hold on, Jake. *Norway*?'

'Yeah. We'd been there for a week, we were playing Trondheim with Gilles de Rais in support.'

Damn. She should have realised before now that the Black Count couldn't have been the killer. She throbbed with disappointment and frustration.

'You can prove this?'

'Of course I can. Ask Tarq. Or Pete – he was driving the tour bus.'

Sophie stepped a little closer to the Count, her breath sweet and hot on his face.

'Would you like me to suck you off, Jake?'

She heard the Count's breathing quicken.

'I'll go crazy if you don't.'

'You'd like me to kneel down and take your pretty cock into my mouth?'

'Do it. Do it now, please. I can't hold out much longer, you've no idea.'

'You've wasted my time, Jake. I ought to punish you for that. In fact, I think I shall.'

Turning on her heel, she stalked across to the door and opened it. For a moment she felt a twinge of regret. He was a very pretty boy under all that black and white make-up, and she could quite relish the taste of his jism on her tongue. But in her heart of hearts, she knew that ordinary pleasure was the last thing the Black Count needed.

'Come back – look, this game's gone on long enough.'

Opening the door, Sophie turned to look at the Count.

'Game? What game?'

'You can't leave me like this!' The Count's cock danced in the excitement of his bondage. He had never been so aroused in his whole life. 'You can't.'

'Oh but I can,' replied Sophie softly; and letting the door close behind her, she walked away along the darkened passage.

Two days later, Zoë Mellenger came to the Hall to see Sophie.

Sophie ushered her into Andre's office.

'I hope you've had better luck than I have.'

Zoë took a seat and opened her briefcase.

'You haven't found out anything?'

'Let's say I've eliminated a few of our suspects, but nothing more.'

'No dark secrets?'

'Plenty – but not about Andre. How about you?'

Zoë sat back in her chair and crossed her legs.

'Well . . . I didn't want to say anything before, because I wasn't sure I was right, but . . .'

'But what?'

'You know Laszlo's employing me to look for Trixie?'

Sophie nodded.

'What's that got to do with Andre's murder?'

'That card Andre received the day before he died – you remember, the one with the pink heart on it? I thought it rang a bell, so I did a little spadework. Seems it came from a company which hires out luxury limousines.'

'So?'

'*So*, the principal shareholder in the company is Lady Anastasia Madeley.'

Chapter 11

Lady Anastasia Madeley toyed with the enormous solitaire diamond on her wedding finger.

'Naturally, a limousine hire firm isn't the calibre of business venture I would normally become involved with.'

'But?' ventured Sophie.

'But, darling, I received it as part of one of my divorce settlements. And one doesn't look a gift horse in the mouth, does one?'

Sophie glanced around the walls of Lady Anastasia's luxurious sitting room. It was the National Gallery in miniature: Impressionist, Ethnic, Naive, Renaissance, Art Nouveau – it struck Sophie that there had been a lot of gift horses in Lady Madeley's life.

'I'm sure *you* don't,' Sophie commented drily.

Lady Anastasia did not rise to the bait.

'Anyway, after you'd contacted me I decided to do a little investigation myself.'

'Really?' Sophie put down her coffee cup. 'And what did you discover?'

'I visited the firm unannounced – it's so much more interesting that way. And do you know what I found?'

'Tell me.'

'I found the managing director and his secretary sitting in his office, *enjoying* a set of naughty videos he'd apparently copied from one of the firm's clients.'

'Videos?' Sophie was puzzled. 'This is all very interesting, I'm sure, but how is it relevant?'

Lady Madeley allowed the beginnings of a smug smile to creep around the corners of her mouth.

'Allow me to demonstrate, darling. I'm sure you'll agree that they are *very* relevant.'

Picking up a remote handset, she switched on the video player. As the blurred screen cleared, resolving itself into moving pictures, even Sophie had to admit that Lady Anastasia was right.

'That's . . . that's . . .'

'Yes, Sophie dear, it's you with a couple of . . . friends. Very good friends by the look of it. And look, the next sequence shows Andre, and *he's* got a friend with him too. Pretty little thing, isn't she?'

Sophie seethed, but said nothing. She reminded herself that her purpose in coming here was to gain information, not take her anger out on Anastasia Madeley – however much she might deserve it.

'I think I have seen quite enough,' snapped Sophie.

Anastasia clicked off the VCR and the screen went blank.

'Darling,' she purred. 'I always thought you were nothing but a cheap tart Paolo Ceretto picked up out of the gutter. I had no idea you were so sophisticated in your tastes, so . . . adventurous.'

The triumphal sneer on Anastasia Madeley's face was too much for Sophie to stand. Anastasia reeked of privilege, whereas she had had to learn her whoring the hard way, striving against all the odds to make something of her life.

She stood up slowly, her hands clenching and unclenching.

'Say that again, bitch.'

Anastasia did not rise from her chair. She simply uncrossed her long, sleek thighs.

'Say what, darling? That you're a cheap little guttersnipe who's no better than she ought to be? It'd be my pleasure.'

At that moment Sophie's self-control snapped. Drawing back her right hand, she dealt Anastasia a stinging slap across the face. Anastasia did not flinch. Her eyes sparkling with some secret excitement, she rose to her feet and returned Sophie's slap with a vicious backhander across the cheek.

'Two can play at that game, darling.'

For a moment Sophie's head spun. Then rage and resentment took over, and she flew at Anastasia, her fingers becoming claws which tore at her clothes, bruising and scratching.

Anastasia fought back, ripping Sophie's blouse as they fell to the ground in a tangled heap of arms and legs. Sophie felt Anastasia's teeth in her shoulder, biting right through her blouse.

'You vicious cow . . .'

With strength she hardly knew she had, Sophie drew up

her knees and kicked out hard, her feet landing square in Anastasia's stomach and sending her flying. She sprawled on the carpet, her skirt up round her elegant backside. Sophie sprang at her, pushing her down hard, straddling her with her thighs.

'So you think you're better than me? You think you can say anything and get away with it because I'm some kind of brainless whore?'

'Darling,' breathed Anastasia. 'You should take it as a compliment. You *know* I'd never want to *hurt* you.'

For an instant Sophie was puzzled. What was this? What game was Anastasia playing – one minute the high-and-mighty lady of the manor, the next a spitting fury, and now a high-class tease? Then something clicked. A look in Anastasia's eyes. A look that begged and pleaded . . .

Sophie laughed and kept on laughing. Still pinning Anastasia to the carpet, she took her left nipple between finger and thumb and pinched it, very hard. Anastasia closed her eyes and a whisper of delicious agony escaped from between her parted lips.

'You desire me, don't you, Anastasia? You want me to do things to you, things that only another woman can do?'

Anastasia did not reply, but Sophie heard her panting softly, and felt her hips gyrating slowly between her thighs, moving to the rhythm of her need.

'You want me to lick you out? Fuck you?' Sophie reached out and picked up a bronze Deco statuette from a side table. 'Bugger you with this?'

Anastasia's face mingled fear, excitement, the delicious depravity of guilty desire.

'Yes,' she whispered.

Sophie thought of leaving her there, sprawled on the floor; yes, leaving her there in the shame of her submission. That would be a victory she might enjoy. And yet . . . and yet, she had come to Lady Anastasia's house looking for information and she had still to obtain it. Sex was the best method of persuasion she knew.

'If you want it, I'm going to give it to you,' she smiled. 'Hard.'

Anastasia's Catherine Walker blouse ripped with a satisfying whisper of torn silk. Underneath she was wearing an underwired half-cup bra which left her nipples teasingly bare. They were smaller than Sophie had anticipated, but she could remedy that. She could make them swell into wood-hard pegs of flesh, obscenely protruberant and begging to be tormented.

Sophie took one into her mouth, the other between finger and thumb. She began by licking and stroking, with a featherlight touch which quickly reduced Anastasia to helpless moans of desire. Her body writhed, snake-like, between Sophie's thighs and, in spite of herself, Sophie felt the first awakenings of desire.

At the first savage bite Anastasia let out a tearing cry.

'Noooo!'

Exhilaration gripped Sophie.

'Yes, bitch. Yes. You wanted this, you still want it. You will take whatever I choose to give you.'

Sucking and biting, pinching and rolling, Sophie drew out Anastasia's nipples until they were long, hard, blush-red stalks whose tips were so hypersensitive that the slightest brush of Sophie's tongue-tip made Anastasia beg for mercy.

She slid down Anastasia's body and pulled her thighs apart, slipping between them.

'You're a disgusting little tart,' sniffed Sophie. 'Your pants are soaking wet.'

The frilly white panties were soaked through at the crotch, making the fabric so diaphanous that Sophie could clearly make out the dusky pink frills of Anastasia's inner labia, and the darker pink oval which marked the deep well of her sex.

'Disgusting, depraved little bitch. I shall have to punish you, you know.'

The panties yielded willingly to the slightest persuasion, and slid off easily, aided by Anastasia who lifted her backside as Sophie tore at them.

'You want it, don't you?'

Anastasia moaned and murmured a few indecipherable syllables.

'Don't you?' Sophie's sharp-nailed finger skated over the glossy wetness of Anastasia's quim. 'And you'd better tell me quickly, or I shall leave you exactly like this.'

'No, please . . .'

'Well?'

'Yes.' The word rushed out in a luxurious sigh. 'Yes, I want it. I want you to do it to me.'

Unseen by Anastasia, Sophie reached out and picked up one of her gloves from the table. It was hand-sewn from the finest textured leather, quite rough to the touch.

She slipped it on her right hand. She was certain that Anastasia would appreciate it.

'What do you want me to do, bitch?'

'I want you to make me come. I want you to . . . fuck me.'

Her words ended in a long, trembling sigh and Sophie saw juices coursing from Anastasia's sex, trickling over her thighs and dripping on the exquisite Afghan carpet beneath her.

Sophie did not speak. Her reply was to plunge her index finger deep into the heart of Anastasia's womanhood. She sighed, moaned, pushed herself down on the finger as though it were a miniature penis.

'Yes. Oh yes, that feels so good.'

'Not as good as this will feel.'

A second finger, a third, a fourth – and Sophie's entire hand was inside Anastasia's sex, curling itself into a fist. Now Anastasia was afraid; afraid of the terrible, tearing pleasure which held her prisoner.

'No!'

'Yes, Anastasia. Yes.'

'No please – please don't!'

Sophie began fisting her. She paid no attention to gentleness, guessing that Anastasia would not thank her for it. She was dealing with a woman who had been with hundreds of men, done everything . . . or thought she had.

'Tell me, bitch.'

'I . . . don't . . . understand.'

The fist fucked harder, faster.

'Tell me the name.'

'Please!'

'The name of the client who hired the limo, bitch. Tell me now.'

'I don't know. I ... swear ... I ... don't ... know.' Anastasia's breath came with difficulty now. She was riding a rollercoaster of terrible, awesome pleasure. 'Whoever it was ... they ... didn't give a name.'

Damn you, thought Sophie, ramming hard with her fist, taking out all her anger and frustration on this arrogant, condescending, captivating woman. Innocent too ... she'd stake money on the fact that she was telling the truth. Would she never find out who killed Andre?

And then ... and then, as Anastasia screamed and her sex muscles clenched in ecstasy, Sophie had an idea. She wondered why it hadn't occurred to her before. There was only one place that videotape could have come from. Only one person who could be behind it.

Davina Templeton.

Sophie was white-hot with anger, an avenging angel.

It was late when she stormed into Satin Miss, but she knew that Davina would still be there. Of course she would. Davina was so *conscientious* about her work, everyone knew that. Bitch, bitch, bitch, Sophie muttered under her breath. Her face was cold with sweat, her hands trembling. Rational thought had deserted her long ago. Now all she could think about was revenge.

Where was she? Where was the bitch who had tried to

destroy her? She would give her a lesson in destruction that she would never forget.

Davina was working late in the office when Sophie stormed in, kicking the door open so hard that the door handle left a dent in the wall.

'Sophie? Is something wrong?'

'Wrong? You'd know all about that, wouldn't you, you treacherous slut?'

'W-what? Bloody hell, Sophie, what do you think you're doing – aah!'

Davina yelped with pain as Sophie seized her by her hair and, twisting it into a rope, used it to drag her out of her chair.

'You're coming with me, Davina. There are things you're going to tell me about. Things you've been hiding from me.'

'Look, I don't understand . . .'

'Shut it! Shut up. You'll talk when I say so, and not before.'

Sophie hardly recognised the steely edge in her own voice as she dragged the protesting Davina out of the office, along the corridor and up the stairs into the attic punishment room. Her own strength astonished her. She supposed it must be true that extreme anger could turn you into some kind of superhuman creature. At any rate, no matter how hard Davina struggled she could not pull away from Sophie's iron grip.

The door of the punishment room slammed shut. Sophie looked at Davina, saw the fear in her eyes and realised that she had been wanting to do this for a long,

long time. She had never liked Davina. Never trusted her. Only now, she had a reason to hate her.

She tied her up, chaining her wrists to an iron ring set high in the wall and manacling her ankles so that she could not kick out.

'Why are you doing this, Sophie?' Davina's eyes followed Sophie as she picked up a pair of sharp-bladed shears.

'You know exactly why.' She cut through Davina's clothes from neck to hem and they fell away, exposing bare flesh. The blades glinted in the sinister, wintry light from the single barred window. 'You're going to tell me the truth for once in your miserable life.'

'Truth? What truth? You're insane, Sophie, do you know that?'

The flat of the scissor blade caught her across the thigh and she gasped at the discomfort.

'Don't lie to me. I know about the tape.'

'The . . .?'

'I know you were involved in Andre's death. I know about the video recordings you made. I know about the limousine.'

Davina's lip curled into a defiant sneer.

'If you know so much, what do you need me for?'

Davina's defiance was cut short as Sophie seized her nipples and twisted them hard. Her eyes closed. Confusion filled her. *Pain, pleasure; pleasure, pain; which was which?* She wasn't sure any more. Had she really changed so much?

'Now. The truth,' hissed Sophie.

A voice behind her froze the scene into a bizarre tableau.

'I think you'd better stop that, Sophie, before you do something you're going to regret.'

Heart pounding, Sophie swung round. Laszlo Comaneci was standing in the doorway. She opened her mouth to turn on him too, but he spoke first.

'Dee-Dee told me something was going on. I think you'd better explain.'

'Davina is just about to confess to me that she was involved in Andre's death.'

'She's crazy!' protested Davina, tugging at the chains which bound her. 'Don't listen to her, Laszlo, the bitch is off her head. I always knew you should never have got involved with the stupid slut.'

Laszlo suppressed a smile. There was something at once erotically stimulating and amusing about the sight of two beautiful she-cats spitting hatred at each other.

'Be quiet, both of you.' Laszlo's voice commanded obedience. 'And for God's sake let's be rational about this. Sophie, untie Davina. Davina, when I want your advice I'll ask for it.'

Sophie complied with a bad grace, unlocking the manacles and throwing the key on the floor.

'Satisfied?'

'Not quite. I want to know what makes you think Davina is involved in Andre's death.'

'Anastasia Madeley showed me video films which I believe were used to blackmail him. They could have been made only by someone who knew us both intimately.' She flung Laszlo's PA a look of loathing. 'Someone like Davina.'

Laszlo nodded.

'I can see your point,' he conceded.

Davina stared at him in horror.

'Laszlo, how could you!'

He silenced her with a look.

'As I said, I can see your point. But however misguided Davina can sometimes be, she's no liar. If she tells you she wasn't involved, she wasn't.'

Sophie thumped the table in frustration.

'But Laszlo, there's no one else it could be. No one!'

'Oh yes there is,' replied Laszlo. And he proceeded to tell her exactly who.

Stephanie Lace had just stepped out of a nice, relaxing shower and was starting to pack her possessions into tea chests and boxes. She'd decided the best thing to do was sub-let her flat and move out of the area. It was too dangerous to stay here any longer.

The sound of the doorbell surprised her. She wasn't expecting any visitors this evening – but maybe it was Mrs Thompson, come to collect her cleaning money. She stood up and stretched, easing on a soft towelling bathrobe over her nakedness.

Opening the door, she encountered not Mrs Thompson but Zoë Mellenger. It took quite a lot of effort to appear unconcerned.

'Zoë! How nice of you to call. I wasn't expecting you.'

Zoë looked Stephanie up and down.

'No. I can see that. Can I come in?'

Without waiting for Stephanie's reply, she pushed into the flat, leaving the front door slightly ajar.

'I . . . er . . .' floundered Stephanie. 'Would you like a coffee or something? A glass of wine?'

'No, nothing.' Zoë contemplated the open suitcases, the jumble of clothes scattered all over the floor, the newspaper packages stuffed into tea chests and trunks. 'Thinking of going somewhere?'

'I'm moving. To Aberdeenshire. A friend's got a business there.'

'I see. Rather sudden isn't it?'

'I've been thinking about it for ages.'

'You mean, you've been thinking about it since Andre Grafton died.'

Stephanie's breath caught in her throat.

'What do you mean?'

'I mean, Stephanie, that you know something about Andre's death, and you're scared stiff somebody's going to catch on and ask you some awkward questions.'

'That's rubbish, I . . .'

'Well I've caught on, Stephanie, and I'm going to ask you those questions. So tell me – how were you involved in Doctor Grafton's death? Screwing you, was he? Did he tell you it was all over and you decided to get your own back? Or were you just jealous of all those gorgeous female patients he used to fuck in his consulting room?'

'Stop it!' Stephanie put her hands over her ears. 'I won't listen. And I won't tell you anything, either.' She pouted like a child. 'You can't make me.'

'But *I* can,' hissed Sophie, pushing open the sitting-room door and walking in. 'Can't I, Stephanie?'

'Sophie! I . . .'

'You wouldn't lie to me, would you Stephanie? You wouldn't dare.'

She was dressed to kill: a she-devil in high-heeled thigh boots, leather miniskirt and tight-laced leather basque. Black was the colour of her vengeance, and a huge black diamond swung, glittering, in the deep valley between her breasts.

Stephanie took a step back.

'Sophie, you've got it all wrong.'

'I don't think so.' Sophie's pursuit of her quarry was unhurried, almost leisurely. She had all the time in the world. Stephanie Lace wasn't going anywhere. 'Did you really think you could get away with it?'

Stephanie was shaking. But still she tried to deny it.

'I haven't done anything, I haven't!'

Her back was up against the wall and Sophie was right in front of her, her blue eyes blazing cold fire. Her hand seized the front of Stephanie's robe and tore it open, revealing the chilled white flesh beneath.

'Tell me what you know.'

Stephanie gasped as a glossy black nail scored a thin trail of crimson beads across her breast.

'I didn't mean it, Sophie! I didn't mean any harm, I swear it.'

Zoë Mellenger shook her head sadly and, taking Sophie by the shoulder, drew her gently away.

'Oh, Stephanie, what have you done?'

Stephanie slid, utterly exhausted, into one of the arm-chairs.

'I made the videotapes, that's all.'

'Why?'

'Because I've always wanted to work on a newspaper, and someone said they could give me a break.'

'Someone? Who?' snapped Sophie.

'A journo on one of the tabloids. The *Comet*. He said if I could dig some dirt on you and Doctor Grafton, send him some juicy videos, he'd print an exposé and share the byline with me.'

Sophie gave a dry laugh.

'And I suppose you were more than happy to oblige? Really, Stephanie, you sicken me.'

'Go on, Stephanie,' said Zoë, motioning to Sophie to be quiet.

'I got the tapes and sent them to him. A few days later, I heard that Doctor Grafton was dead.' She put her head in her hands and started sobbing. 'I didn't know what would happen, I didn't.'

'Come on, Stephanie,' cut in Zoë. 'Pull yourself together. Who did you send these tapes to?'

Stephanie sniffed and wiped her eyes.

'To tell you the truth I'm not sure. You see, the journo *said* he was with the *Comet*, but he wanted me to send the tapes to his house. Later on, I found out that no one at the *Comet* had ever heard of him.'

'Who?' demanded Sophie. She wasn't sure what answer she was expecting to hear, but it certainly wasn't the one she got.

Stephanie's voice trembled as she spoke the name.

'I don't know if it's his real name. But he calls himself Emil Bernhardt.'

Chapter 12

Emil Bernhardt could hardly believe his good fortune.

Sophie Ceretto had telephoned him out of the blue and asked him if he'd like to go riding with her. Emil congratulated himself on his skill; he hadn't expected Sophie to come across quite so easily. Maybe she'd relied on Andre more than he'd thought. But whatever the reason for her sudden compliance, he'd succeeded in opening her up like a flower... and way ahead of schedule.

A light mist of warm drizzle filled the air as Emil saddled up and followed Sophie out of the stable yard, but nothing could spoil this for him. He reined in his mount, letting her get a little way ahead so that he could enjoy looking at her for a while.

Sophie was dressed with a kind of alluring primness which only she could make sexy. She was wearing the full Victorian-style riding habit: a hat with a veil which flew out behind her as she rode; a ruffle-necked white shirt beneath a sharply tailored green jacket, and a long black divided skirt. To add to the curious period ambience, she was riding side-saddle, her pretty patent-leather boots balanced delicately on the foot-rest, revealing a tantalising inch or two of silk-stockinged ankle.

Emil could feel his juices flowing. What a tart she was beneath that little-miss-prim veneer. And he knew full well that it was nothing more than a veneer: after all, he had seen the films. He amused himself by fantasising about what she would be wearing underneath that riding habit: period underwear perhaps? A lacy camisole and knee-length calico drawers, split wide open at the quim? Tight-laced stays? Or perhaps something really sluttish – a red nylon peephole bra and crotchless panties. Now *that* would be a present worth unwrapping.

Spurring on his horse, he drew level with her.

'What do you think of the estate?'

She turned her face towards him, her lips very glossy and kissable.

'Very impressive. Is all this land yours?'

Emil surveyed the broad horizon.

'Everything as far as that hill to the south, and the windmill over there. Five thousand acres in all.'

'You must be even wealthier than I thought,' commented Sophie slyly. 'I had no idea the wages of sin were so high.'

'And what, precisely, is that supposed to mean?'

'Whatever you want it to mean.'

Laughing, she flicked the reins and the horse cantered off across the fields. Emil set off in pursuit, not too eager to catch up because he enjoyed a chase and wanted to make it last.

Sophie's horse sailed gracefully over a five-barred gate,

but it wasn't the horse Emil was looking at. He was admiring Sophie's wonderfully rounded arse, and the totally irresistible way her breasts leapt and quivered inside her tight jacket. She must have chosen that outfit knowing what it would do to him, fully aware that it moulded her body like the tightest and most sensual embrace.

There was no doubt about it: every movement of Sophie's delectable body was a conscious attempt to drive him wild. That was probably how she got her kicks, making men wet their pants over her. His cock twitched in his jodhpurs and he licked his lips. If that was how she wanted to play it, he was only too happy to go along with the game.

'Come here, you little vixen,' he called out, galloping ahead of her and turning his horse so that he stood across her path and she was obliged to pull up short.

'Why?' teased Sophie, her red lips pouting defiance.

'Because I want to teach you a lesson for insulting me.'

'Come on then. If you're man enough.'

Emil leapt down from the saddle, sliding his riding crop through his belt. He knew his powerful body looked good in his skintight jodhpurs, riding boots and open-necked shirt. How could Sophie Ceretto resist him? In any case, he had no intention of letting her.

Just as he was about to grab her, she moved to lift her riding crop. But Emil was too quick for her, seizing the reins and holding the horse firm.

'Trying to run away from me?'

'Why should I want to do that?' She ran the tip of her

tongue over her lips, slowly and salaciously.

'Who knows? Perhaps you're afraid of what I might do to you.'

Sophie's blue eyes traced a lingering path down his chest and belly to the thick diagonal swelling of his erect penis. She smiled impishly.

'Afraid? Darling, I don't see *anything* to be afraid of.'

This was too much for Emil. He grabbed hold of her wrist and, with a swift jerk, unseated her from the side-saddle. She gave a soft squeal of protest and wriggled a little in his grasp, but all in all it was pretty obvious to Emil that Sophie Ceretto was every bit as much of a slut as he'd been led to believe. She was desperate for it.

They tussled in the drizzle, play-fighting; Sophie determined not to surrender *too* easily. But Emil was strong and Sophie was willing. It was a simple matter to overpower her and send her skidding down into the mud.

'Beast!' she spat.

'Vixen,' he growled, and sprang at her.

She wriggled like a mudhopper in his grasp, her riding habit sodden with slimy greenish-black mud. But Emil had no intention of letting her escape him. He flipped her over on to her belly. She twisted her face round to hurl obscenities at him; it was covered with muddy patches, like warpaint, giving her the air of beautiful and lascivious savage.

'I'm going to teach you a lesson you won't forget in a hurry,' he told her, fiddling in the muddy mess for the button which fastened Sophie's riding skirt at the waist.

'Bastard,' she hissed. He had never heard that word

pronounced with such lust before. She could have murmured, 'Fuck me like a bitch in season, darling,' and it could not have sounded sexier.

Emil succeeded at last in unfastening the row of buttons and she was his. Pinning her down with his thighs, he wrenched down the skirt, not quite knowing what he might find underneath. Calico drawers, red nylon crotchless panties, a black fur g-string . . .

Or simply . . . nothing. If you could call Sophie Ceretto's creamy backside nothing.

'You slut. You darling slut,' he murmured. Oh but she had heavenly arse-cheeks, rounded and smooth and as firm and pale as fresh cream cheese. How could any redblooded man resist them?

He withdrew the riding crop from his belt. The stock felt hot, as though his own urgent passion had communicated itself to it. He ran the looped tip over Sophie's cheek.

'You know what I'm going to do, Sophie? I'm going to punish you for being a filthy-minded slut. You're an indisciplined filly, and I intend to bring you to heel.'

She made a half-hearted attempt to wriggle free, but Emil felt her shudder with excitement as the riding crop teased and tickled its way over her bare thighs and drew invisible patterns on her upraised backside.

Invisible – but not for long. Without warning, Emil drew back the riding crop and let fly with the first slicing blow. It flicked diagonally across both buttocks, and Sophie leapt and cursed and squirmed in the slippery mud. But she betrayed her passion with a soft sigh, and seemed to thrust out her backside as though begging for more.

Emil Bernhardt was not one to let a lady down. He beat her with rhythmic precision, thrilling to the sight of her martyred backside, crisscrossed with blush-red stripes. He took care not to break the skin; he was no sadist, just a country gentleman with a love of well-trained fillies. What's more, it excited and aroused him to know that Sophie was enjoying the experience every bit as much as he was.

At last her backside was exactly the way he wanted it: two flame-red circles, a little swollen from the thorough whipping and radiating a special kind of heat. As he ran his cool hands over her buttocks, Sophie let out little whimpers, but this time she made no attempt to resist his determined desires. On the contrary, she drew herself up on to hands and knees, forcing her buttocks into his hands, encouraging him to do exactly what he wanted . . . to seize and squeeze them, to pull them apart, to expose the hot, wet heartland of her sex.

The puckered kiss of her anus seemed to pout at him, inviting him in; but it was the beauty of Sophie's pussy which overwhelmed him. It smelt spicy and honeysweet, and like an exotic flower it trickled and oozed with nectar.

His dick seemed to pound with the pulse of his need. Swiftly he unzipped his jodhpurs, slipped his hand inside his shorts and took it out. It felt huge, disembodied, so monstrous in the strength of its desire that it had taken on a life of its own. *Fuck her, fuck her, fuck her*, it seemed to scream at him. And he had not the slightest motivation to resist.

He took her with a triumphant cry, riding her as though she were some thoroughbred mare; paying no attention to her pleasure but pursuing his own with a sort of crazy compulsion. The walls of her sex were so slippery with juice that their caress was featherlight, despite its tightness, and his fucking seemed endless; wonderful but unsatisfying. He had to come, she was denying him, he must and would fill her with his spunk, he would, he would . . .

Suddenly and almost imperceptibly, Sophie tightened her pussy muscles. It was the smallest of movements, yet its effect on Emil was immense. All at once, the full power of a thousand different, exquisite sensations bore down upon him, engulfed and surrounded him, drowning him in pleasure.

With a final thrust, his prick jerked and the first creamy spurt of semen jetted out of him. Emil fell forward on Sophie's back, clawing at her in the frenzy of his passion, for a few seconds completely helpless as his orgasm took him over.

He withdrew from her, and pearly fluid trickled thickly from her swollen, blossoming sex, forming an opalescent slick on her upper thighs. She knelt in silent stillness, obedient now. Emil traced the curve of her backside. *His* now. His body to do with whatever he liked.

'Roll over and lie on your back, Sophie.'

She did so.

'Like this?' Her voice was thick and husky with excitement. Emil wondered if she had climaxed; he hadn't thought to ask. And in any case, it was his pleasure that mattered, not hers.

'Open your mouth.'

A couple of flicks of the wrist and he was stiff again already. Sophie's mouth, wet-lipped and appealing, offered itself to him and he accepted the offer with alacrity.

'Take it. Take it in. *Right* in.'

He had no need to chastise her, which disappointed him slightly. Sophie opened wide and swallowed him down, winding her tongue wickedly about the root of his dick. He gasped. She was good. Even better than he'd expected.

'Squeeze my balls.'

Her fingers curled themselves about his testicles and began squeezing and stroking them, with such mischievous skill that Emil wondered just how long he was going to be able to hold himself in.

'Suck me now. Hard. And mind you don't bite me, or I shall have to whip you again.'

He felt her teeth graze his shaft very, very lightly, as though she were teasing him and daring him to punish her again. Perhaps that was exactly what she wanted him to do. He drove into her again and again, trying not just to bring himself off but to subdue her. But those blue eyes sparkled insolently as those rosy lips sucked long and hard, drawing him on and on and on.

If only he could make it last for ever. Make Sophie go on sucking and licking and squeezing and caressing until his brain spun with the effort of not coming. If only . . . but what did it matter? They had all day and Emil intended to make the most of it.

Oh Paolo, he thought with a silent chuckle. *Paolo*

Ceretto, you're deceiving yourself if you think I'm handing this one over to you. This one's all mine.

Side by side, Emil and Sophie rode slowly back to the house, sticky and caked with mud. Sophie's chuckle was low and sexy.

'Whatever will people say when they see us looking like this?'

Emil's smile was tight-lipped.

'They wouldn't dare say anything,' he replied. 'My staff are too well-trained to be that stupid.'

'You're very... masterful,' observed Sophie archly. She reached across and ran her hand up his thigh. His jodhpurs were absolutely sodden with mud, and the wet fabric clung to his flesh, revealing the appetisingly firm lines of his muscular legs.

He seized her hand, and carried it to his lips.

'They say power is the perfect aphrodisiac.'

'It certainly works for me.'

At the entrance to the stable yard they dismounted. A young groom appeared from nowhere, silently took the reins and – without so much as a word or a curious glance – led the horses away.

'Come into the house.' Emil's hands encircled Sophie's waist and slid down to the wet riding skirt, which had stuck to her backside and sculpted the line of her round bum-cheeks with perfect artistry. 'I'll find you some clean clothes.'

Sophie laughed.

'I think I could use a bath first.'

Emil glanced at his Rolex.

'Tomkins is already running you one.'

If Sophie was surprised she did not show it. Why should she be surprised by anything that Emil Bernhardt did, or knew, or thought? She followed him into the house. It was certainly impressive – just like Emil Bernhardt's technique. She looked around her, estimating how many millions it would cost to buy a place like this. Nice. The man had taste.

'Has the estate been in your family a long time?'

'Hardly. I bought it a couple of years ago, when my accountant thought I had a little too much spare cash.'

'Really? I thought . . .'

'Money can buy anything,' said Emil. His hand smoothed down over Sophie's moist backside. '*Anything*. That's something you need to know if you want real success.'

'Oh, I'm sure you could teach me a lot.'

'More than you could guess.'

A butler greeted them with a silver tray and two glasses of hot rum punch.

'Try it,' nodded Emil. 'It'll . . . warm you up.'

Sophie reached out for it but at the last moment something in her brain said no. She shook her head.

'Later maybe.'

'As you wish.' She noticed that he sounded faintly annoyed. Emil snapped his fingers at the butler. 'We are not to be disturbed, is that clear?'

'Perfectly, sir.'

Emil switched back on that famous, lustful smile, and

Sophie felt desire rekindling inside her as he led her up the broad, sweeping staircase.

The master bedroom was at the rear of the house, with huge bay windows which overlooked acres of formal gardens laid out by Capability Brown. As Sophie was gazing out of the window, Emil slid smoothly up behind her and pressed his body against her back.

'You're cold.'

She wriggled her backside against the flat muscle of Emil's belly, feeling a burgeoning hardness at its root.

'Not for long.'

'Not if I have anything to do with it.'

All thoughts of their bath suddenly forgotten, his hands slid upward and cupped her breasts. She leaned slightly forward, balancing her elbows on the windowsill, and the full weight of her breasts fell into his palms.

'You're such a slut, Sophie.' There was a growl of admiration in Emil's voice. 'I think I could screw you all day and all night, and still come back for more.'

She responded by pushing against his dick, grinding hard, rubbing him with a subtle skill. His dick-tip, closely moulded by his wet jodhpurs, slipped into the crack between her buttocks, and she held it there, her hands pushing her bum-cheeks together so that they encircled it.

He moved with her in long, slow strokes, not quite sure if he was using her to bring himself off, or if she was using him to gratify some impish whim. He whispered obscenities as he nuzzled her neck, exciting himself as he rubbed his cock smoothly up and down the wet, muddy furrow of her bum-crease.

'Bitch, hot bitch. I'm going to fuck you, I'm going to shag you senseless. I'm going to strip you and tie you up and fuck you till you can't take any more . . .'

Urgent hands wrenched down her mud-soaked riding skirt, tearing off the buttons in their hurry to strip the wet material away from the flesh. Underneath, Sophie's bum-cheeks were cold and moist, pearly-white beneath their caking of semi-dried mud.

He grabbed her by the arse and pulled her open. She was still wet with his spendings, and glossy with the abundant wetness of her own sluttish desire. It was obvious that she wanted it, she was pushing out that breathtaking backside and moaning softly. Her breasts were soft and wet in his hands as he pushed his dick between her bum-cheeks and drove into her.

'Yes, yes, yes,' he heard her moan. Encouraged by her obvious pleasure, he drove into her faster. Her hips were moving from side to side now, and he knew what Sophie was doing. She was rubbing her shaven quim against the ornate Edwardian radiator beneath the window, using it to stimulate her clitoris. What a versatile slut she was: able to find pleasure anywhere, anyhow. What a find. What an acquisition she was going to make.

A voice behind him interrupted his pleasure with brutal coldness. It was floating up the stairs from the ground floor.

'Bernhardt.'

He paused, half-turned, and called out, 'Go away. I'm busy.'

'You're needed.'

'Whatever it is, it'll keep.'

'Get down here *now*, Bernhardt. It's business. *Urgent* business, understand?'

Emil sighed. Bugger it. But there were some people you didn't say no to. Not if you valued your bollocks. Reluctantly he withdrew.

'I have to go.'

Sophie rolled round to face him, leaning coquettishly against the windowsill. She pouted.

'Now? Can't you stay just a little longer?'

'It's something I have to deal with right away. Listen, why don't you take a bath and ... you know ... get ready for me?' He winked as he kissed her. 'I'll get Tomkins to send a maid up to help you slip into something warm and welcoming.'

As the door closed behind him, Sophie breathed a sigh of relief. She was beginning to wonder how much longer she could keep up this charade. She hoped that whatever Emil's urgent business was, it would keep him out of her hair for a while. What she'd really like to do now was get bathed, dressed and out of this place before Emil came back for round two – if possible, taking with her a tasty titbit or two of useful information.

She had washed her hair and was just sliding into the huge sunken bath when there was a knock at the door. Damn. It must be the maid.

'Come in.'

The bathroom door opened and a blonde girl in a French maid's outfit teetered into the room on four-inch red high heels. Her fishnet stockings stopped a good two inches below the hem of her frilly white petticoat, and her enormous breasts threatened to burst out of her black, low-cut maid's dress.

'Sophie!' squealed the maid. 'Sophie, it's *you*!'

Sophie was so astonished that she had to take a second look. Then a third.

'Trixie? *Trixie*!'

Trixie giggled and perched herself on the rim of the bath. Nobody giggled like that. Nobody filled a dress like that. Nobody had bouncy blonde curls and candy-pink lips. Nobody but Trixie.

'Of course it's me, silly.' Sophie noticed that Trixie was giggling even more than usual. Despite the bizarre clothes, and everyone being worried frantic about her disappearance, Trixie seemed . . . happy. Unnaturally happy. Those round blue eyes seemed more vacant than Sophie recalled, almost . . . glazed. Sophie remembered the butler with the glass of hot rum punch. Something had told her not to drink it. She wondered if Trixie had been less cautious . . .

Sophie sat up in the bath, twisting her wet hair up in a towel.

'What on earth are you doing here?'

Trixie trailed her candy-pink nails in the scented bath-water.

'I don't know.' She clapped a hand over her mouth, stifling a tinkle of laughter. 'Isn't that silly?'

'How can you not know? Rick's been really worried about you, don't you realise? And Laszlo.'

'Ricky? And Mr Laszlo?' Trixie put her hand to her forehead as though trying to focus on something half remembered. 'But that doesn't make sense, does it? I mean, Mr Emil said . . .'

'Said what?'

'He said that Mr Laszlo lent me to him for Mr Emil's business, to look after his customers, you know. Only . . . only I don't remember that bit.'

'What *do* you remember?'

Trixie shook her head.

'Just being at the Pink Pearl and then being here. There was something else in between, but I don't remember. I'm such a silly-head, aren't I?'

'Of course you're not. Look.' Sophie began soaping her arms. 'I'm leaving here as soon as I can. Why don't you come back with me?'

'Back?'

'Home with me. Or to the Pink Pearl.'

Trixie looked surprised.

'But, Sophie, I can't. Not if Mr Laszlo says I have to work for Mr Emil.'

'Trixie, you don't understand . . .'

'And anyway,' giggled Trixie. 'It's ever so nice here, I feel all lovely and happy all the time. And so sexy. And Mr Emil's clients are mostly all right, and I get all these new clothes . . .'

'But don't you want to come home?'

Trixie looked at Sophie. For a moment a glimmer of understanding flickered through the blue eyes, then it was gone.

'Home?' A fit of giggles overtook her. 'Oh, Sophie, you are funny! *This* is my home. With Mr Emil.'

* * *

The whip came down with a savage swipe, and Stephanie Lace's head and shoulders were pulled back sharply by the bridle and reins.

It was Sophie who held the reins, Sophie who wielded the whip. She wiped perspiration from her brow with the back of her forearm, before striking Stephanie again, this time across her bare belly. Stephanie whimpered, and drew up her knees.

'You love it, don't you?' hissed Sophie.

'Yeees.'

Swipe.

'You absolutely and utterly adore it.'

'Yes.'

'Say it.'

'I . . . absolutely . . . and utterly . . . adore it.' Stephanie fell back, exhausted, her golden-brown hair plastered to her forehead with sweat, her lightly tanned skin striped here and there with slashes of red.

Sophie threw down the whip. She had no desire to cause Stephanie undue pain, only to bring her under her discipline. And the girl was a novice; it was important not to go too far.

Hands on hips, she contemplated her pupil.

'Spread your legs.'

Stephanie's eyes darkened with fear, but she obeyed. Sophie stretched out her foot and ran the pointed toe of her boot along the deep furrow of Stephanie's pussy. It came away glistening wet with juice.

'You are a slut. Say it.'

Stephanie's voice was a tiny whisper.

'I'm . . . a slut.'

'I can't hear you.' Sophie jabbed her with the toe of her boot. 'Say it. Louder.'

'I'm a slut.'

'Good.' Sophie felt the warmth of relief course through her. Winning over Stephanie was an important part of her plan. 'You are *my* slut, and I am your mistress. Do you understand?'

'Yes, Mistress.'

'Do you wish to prove your loyalty to me?'

'Yes, Mistress.'

'Excellent. Well, I have a task for you to perform, slut. You are going to enter Emil Bernhardt's house and while you are there you will find evidence that he was responsible for Doctor Grafton's death. Do I make myself perfectly clear?'

'Perfectly, Mistress.'

Sophie nodded to Zoë Mellenger, who was watching from a corner. Zoë got to her feet and crossed towards Sophie's trussed and harnessed captive.

'You know Zoë, don't you, slut? She asked you some questions about Andre's death, and you gave her some completely unsatisfactory answers.'

Stephanie hung her head shamefacedly.

'Yes, Mistress.'

'Zoë will brief you on what you are to do. And this time you will always tell her the absolute truth, or you will be severely punished.' Sophie bent down and unbuckled Stephanie's harness. 'You may get up now.'

'Thank you, Mistress.'

'And one more thing, Stephanie.'
She looked up, questioning.
'Mistress?'
'You will not fail me.'

Chapter 13

A man with hands like flat-irons dragged Stephanie up the stairs to Emil Bernhardt's study. She kicked at his shins, scratched at his face, scrabbled with sharpened nails at his Italian mohair suit, but Bernhardt's heavies were well trained. He simply tucked his arm round her waist, lifted her off her feet and carried her the rest of the way.

Bernhardt was transacting a little business via the Internet when the commotion erupted on the landing outside his door. Swiftly logging off, he was just reaching for the handgun he kept in the top drawer of his desk when the door burst open.

'What the . . . you!'

Stephanie glowered at him from beneath a tousled mop of brown hair.

'Yes, Emil. Me. What are you going to do about it?'

'Shut it,' growled the heavy, dropping Stephanie in a heap on Emil's carpet. 'Beggin' your pardon, Mister Bernhardt, sir, only I found this one sniffing around downstairs.'

'Did you now?' Emil slid the desk drawer shut. He got to his feet. 'And what was she up to?'

'Dunno, Mister Bernhardt. Snoopin'.'

Emil surveyed the girl. She was a dishevelled, spitting fury, but not bad-looking for all that.

'OK, you can go. I'll deal with this.'

'Yes, Mister Bernhardt, sir. Me and the boys'll be downstairs if you need us.'

'Just go.'

Bernhardt waited until the sound of footsteps had receded well into the distance before emerging from behind his desk. Stephanie scrambled to her feet, trying to pull her clothing back into some semblance of order. Evidently his bodyguards had had a bit of fun with her before bringing her to him, thought Emil. Actually he rather liked how she looked – she seemed only half civilised, a malevolent little savage in need of breaking.

'Stephanie Lace. Well, well.'

'Surprised to see me?' spat Stephanie.

'Why have you come here?' he demanded coolly.

'I think you know that, *Mister* Bernhardt. You see, it didn't take much effort to find out the truth about you. You don't work for the *Comet* at all, do you? They've never heard of you.'

'Really?' Emil poured himself a drink. 'Do tell me more. It's so fascinating to hear about oneself.'

'In fact you're not a journalist at all, are you? You're just a charlatan who peddles dirty movies. You thought you could use me – you never intended to give me a job at all!'

'Perhaps. Perhaps not.'

Stephanie lowered her voice. It was shaky with anger.

'I've investigated you, Bernhardt. I know *lots* about you. You're shady. What's it worth to you to make sure the information goes no further?'

He looked her up and down. It was obvious the silly girl had no idea of the range of his power, or she'd never dream of presenting him with an ultimatum. He could snap her like a twig, break her and dispose of her and no one would ever be any the wiser. But on the other hand . . . she was a little skinny, it was true. But not ordinary. There was something exotic in those widely spaced, almond-shaped eyes; something very alluring about that overblown rose of a mouth.

'I might have . . . a use for you,' he conceded.

'A job?'

The corners of his mouth twitched slightly, but Stephanie seemed not to have noticed his amusement.

'You might call it that, yes.' He reached beneath the top of his desk and pressed a concealed button.

'What are you doing?'

'Calling for one of my bodyguards.'

Now the almond eyes registered alarm.

'Is this some kind of trick?'

'Not at all.' The door opened and a square-headed man in a black suit appeared, his immense bulk blotting out the light. 'Ah, Jock, take Miss Lace and *help her get ready*. Understood?'

'Understood, Mister Bernhardt, sir.'

Sausage fingers gripped Stephanie's arms and dragged her out towards the stairs.

'Wait!'

Emil nodded and Jock reluctantly stopped.

'What is it, Stephanie?'

'I want to know what this is all about. I want to know what kind of so-called job you're offering me. What's your game, Bernhardt?'

'My *game*, Stephanie? It's no game, I can assure you. I'm in the corporate hospitality business.'

'The . . .' Realisation dawned. 'Oh that's what they're calling it now, is it? Look, Bernhardt, I don't think I want to get involved in anything like this if it's all the same to you . . .'

'Oh but, Stephanie, you're simply perfect for what I have in mind.' Emil's hand gripped her chin, forcing her to look up at him. 'Those slender hands, that generous mouth . . .'

'Let me go!' She wriggled and aimed a swipe at Emil, but he caught her wrist and kissed it.

'Such a little wild cat. Who'd have thought it? It seems I shall have to have you broken in before you can be of any real use to me. You may proceed, Jock. I think I shall settle myself down here and watch.'

Stephanie felt most peculiar.

It had to be some kind of drug that was making her feel like this . . . something they'd put in that glass of mulled wine, perhaps? She shook her head but the feeling of unreality refused to go away. In all honesty, she wasn't sure she wanted it to. It felt kind of . . . nice. Sexy, happy, floaty. Which was odd really, given the rough fucking she'd had from Bernhardt's gorilla of a minder.

222

Funny how mellow she felt about it. Almost grateful . . .

Blinking a few times, she forced herself to focus. She looked down at herself. Was she really wearing this ludicrous costume? Giggles exploded from her and she clapped her hand over her mouth, suddenly afraid that she would never be able to stop.

It was some kind of belly-dancer's outfit, that much at least her fuzzy brain was able to work out. She was wearing gauzy pink pantaloons, tight at the waist and ankle but perfectly sheer everywhere else. Stephanie looked down and noticed that somebody had shaved her. All the golden-brown curls had gone from her mossy knoll and it was naked as a child's. What was more, as she shuffled her feet apart to get a better look, she noticed that the pantaloons were split at the crotch, affording indecent views of her secret parts from pussy to anus.

How shocking! And rather exciting too. Stephanie felt an inescapable warmth spreading all over her body, making it tingle in the most unexpected ways. It wasn't just her nipples that tingled, or the hidden rosebud of her clitoris. No, there were other places that felt aroused too: places that she'd never thought of as erogenous zones.

The backs of her shoulders felt hot and tingly, as though a lover had just planted dozens of tiny kisses there. The whole length of her spine seemed to recall the soft wetness of a tongue, running down from the nape of her neck to the top of the valley which led so deeply between her buttocks. Her arms, her face, her thighs, her belly all tingled and ached with some secret excitement. And with each tiny movement she made, Stephanie's nipples were strangely caressed by the tasselled clips which had been applied to them, teasing them with a delicious sensation of heaviness.

She swayed slightly, and put out a hand to steady herself. At the same moment, her eyes fixed on a group of people somewhere in the middle distance. She forced herself to focus on them. Who were they? And where was she?

A figure detached itself from the group and walked – no, bounced – across to where Stephanie was standing. A girl's face loomed up, a conspiratorial finger pressed to its candy-pink lips.

'W-what?'

The lips framed a soft shushing sound.

'Sssh. You're Stephanie, aren't you?'

Stephanie thought for a moment. Thoughts kept swimming very close, like multicoloured fishes, then at the last moment darting away. It was so frustrating.

'Am I?'

The face giggled and the blue eyes sparkled with merriment. They seemed friendly.

'Of course you are!'

'And who . . . who are you?'

'Me?' The giggles reached a crescendo, the bubbly golden curls bobbing around the face. 'I'm Trixie! Sophie said to take good care of you – but it's a secret. Sssh!'

Sophie? Stephanie racked her brains to work out why that name meant such a lot to her. Why it made her feel so . . . frightened. And excited. And sexy.

'Sophie?'

'Ssssh. Someone might hear. Sophie, you know!'

Stephanie's hand moved automatically to her backside, bare beneath its filmy covering of pink gauze. Some remembered smart came back to her: the sting of the whip; the spreading heat that had begun as pain and ended as pleasure. And she remembered that she had a job to do.

Sophie – of course! Mistress.

Her mind began to clear, and she looked around her, blurred images resolving themselves into clearer pictures. She was standing in a large, ornately decorated room with a deep-pile carpet and a variety of soft sofas. The sofas were adorned by a dozen or so young women dressed in bizarre and very skimpy costumes. Some were giggling, some appeared to be staring blankly into space. Stephanie wondered who they were.

She turned back to Trixie and realised she was rattling on about something. She made an effort to listen – it might be important. Sophie had given her a job to do and she must do it properly, or she would be punished. The thought made her feel excited. It was almost worth risking Sophie's displeasure, just for the pleasure of the punishment.

'Now listen, Stephanie, you *must* listen, it's important.'

'Sorry, Trixie. Go on.'

'You don't want to get beaten, like the other girls, do you?'

Stephanie's gaze drifted to the girls on the sofas.

'They . . . who are they?'

'It's like this, Steph. Mr Emil's clients, well, they like

the girls to give them something special, right?'

'Right.'

'Well, those girls over there, they're ones who've taken a bit longer than usual to learn how to . . . you know . . . *deliver*. You don't want to end up like them, do you?'

'No. Of course not. What do I have to do?'

'Oh, it's not so difficult to please Mr Emil. Just learn quickly and do as you're told. There's the blow-jobs, to start off with. You know how to do them, don't you?'

'I . . . think so.'

Trixie seemed to find this answer hilarious. She erupted into gales of girlish laughter.

'You think so? Of course you do. But when you're doing it for the clients, you have to remember how much they're paying, see? They don't want you making them come in five seconds, do they?'

'I suppose not. But how . . .?'

'Give 'em variety, girl. Suck them off for a bit, then pinch them hard at the tip – like this.' She acted it out for Stephanie. 'See? That way you stop them just before they shoot. Then you can wank them for a while – or let them watch you doing it to yourself. They love that, you know, they really do.'

Stephanie listened in a sort of erotic daze. It all felt vaguely unreal, and yet Trixie's litany of sexual etiquette was curiously arousing too. She imagined herself doing all these things to men who were complete strangers. Could she? Would she?

'Listen,' urged Trixie. 'Don't want to annoy Mr Emil, do you?'

'N-no. No, I don't.'

Trixie nudged her in the ribs.

'Worse than my Ricky-baby he is,' she grinned. 'And *much* worse than Mr Laszlo. He's a gentleman, is Mr Laszlo. Now, there's your arse, Steph, you know how to use it?'

'Use it?'

'To give them pleasure, silly. Get on your hands and knees and let them take you in the arse. Drives them wild it does. And of course, they just *love* giving you a pearl necklace.' Trixie gave Stephanie the once-over, eyeing up her tiny, pert, schoolgirlish breasts. 'Mind you, Steph, you might have a bit of a problem in that department.'

'Hang on a minute, Trixie. A pearl what?'

'A pearl necklace, Steph. A tit-wank. Don't you know *anything*?'

'Sorry, I . . . guess . . . I don't.'

Trixie flipped down the top of her glittery boob tube and two immense melon-shaped breasts leapt out. Stephanie stared at them in astonishment. They were huge, unfeasibly so; their fleshy majesty proudly defying gravity. Long rosy nipples thrust up into the air, making Trixie's monster breasts resemble nothing so much as two tightly knotted party balloons.

'You do it like this, see?' Trixie took a candle from one of the tables and slipped it between her breasts, pushing them together so that they all but engulfed it. 'You just slide your tits up and down his shaft until he spurts. Easy, see! But don't do it too fast . . . you have to make it last, or they're not happy. And then Mr Emil isn't happy.'

'I see.'

Stephanie was doing her best to watch and listen – she knew it was important somehow – but her attention was slipping away. Whatever they'd slipped her in that drink was making her feel so floaty and happy and randy that she felt as if she'd screw the first man who walked in through that door.

Trixie brought her back to herself with a jolt.

'Anyway, good luck, Steph.'

'Good luck? Why do I need good luck?'

Trixie giggled and pointed to the door. One of Emil Bernhardt's bodyguards was beckoning to Steph.

'Mr Emil must think a lot of you, Steph. Looks like you're about to be given your first client.'

It was some days later when Sophie decided to pay Emil Bernhardt a return visit. She wasn't going to make any sudden or unwise moves. Things were already heading her way, and she was content to let the balance of power shift, subtly and by slow degrees, until it tilted in her favour.

Stopping her car just short of the front gates, she took out her powder compact and checked her make-up in the mirror. Nice. Vampishly nice. It was time that Emil Bernhardt came to realise that she was the rapacious one and he was nothing more than a naughty boy. She'd brought some of her toys with her, just to reinforce the point.

Emil was waiting for her in the dining room, with a bottle of Bollinger and a plate of fresh-cream truffles. She could tell he wasn't expecting her to be wearing a fur-trimmed Miss Santa suit in scarlet leather, cut short in the skirt and low in the neck, and laced tight at the waist to throw breasts and buttocks into relief. The flared skirt was short and trimmed with white fur; so short in fact that it revealed her stocking tops, suspenders and fluffy white fur briefs. Fur-trimmed calf-length boots with four-inch heels and a slash of cherry-red lipstick completed the ensemble. It was, to say the least, striking.

Emil's eyes bulged.

'Sophie . . . I . . . don't know what to say.'

Sophie took a truffle from the silver dish, bit into it and licked cocoa powder from her lips.

'Say "thank you", Emil. I've brought you an early Christmas present. Me.'

'I've never seen you like this before.' Emil swallowed. It wasn't like him to be lost for words, but Sophie Ceretto was always a step ahead of him, always ready with some new game-play that left him drooling like a lapdog begging for a chocolate drop.

'There are lots of things I haven't shown you yet. Why don't I start by showing you how nicely I suck cock? Or I could take you between my tits and wank you . . .'

Without so much as a by-your-leave, Sophie planted a passionate kiss on Emil's lips, pushing her tongue inside his mouth. It tasted chocolatey, creamy, alcoholic and very tempting. A growl of appreciative excitement escaped from Emil as he pushed her down on to the crisp white table top.

'I want you, you little vixen. And I'm going to have you. *My* way. Whatever way *I* like.'

'Oh yes,' breathed Sophie, rubbing her belly against Emil's. He was hot and hard for her. 'And you *do* like this, don't you, Emil?'

They rolled over and over across the tablecloth, sending knives, forks and eighteenth-century glassware tumbling and crashing out of the way. Squishy truffles and ripe fruit crushed beneath them, they revelled in the cool wetness, the wickedness of doing just exactly what you pleased.

'We won't be disturbed?' whispered Sophie.

'No. I've given orders.' He fumbled with Sophie's laces, but the costume held firm so he reached into her low-cut bodice and pulled out her breasts, squeezing and biting them as she sprawled on the tablecloth. She responded by sliding her thigh between his legs, drawing it up slowly but firmly until it collided with the softness of his balls, crushing them with a delicious ache. 'Sophie. You bitch. You darling . . .'

The warm glow of success filled Sophie. It was working. Bernhardt simply couldn't get enough. For all his determination to possess and use her, it was she who would use him.

'I can do more,' she breathed.

'Do it.'

She couldn't have wished for more. Turning over very suddenly, she succeeded in rolling them both off the table, dragging the tablecloth with them in a jumble of cutlery and food.

She was on top now. Excellent.

'I'm going to suck you till you beg for mercy,' she told him with a smile. *He thinks I'm joking*, she thought as she looked down at his laughing face. *How little he knows.*

She didn't bother unfastening his flies – she simply took a steak knife and slashed off the buttons. Then tore his trousers and Calvin Kleins down over his hips, baring the tell-tale spike of his over-eager penis.

Her lips encircled it with ravenous delight. He murmured his pleasure and began moving his hips back and forth, as if by forcing his dick further down her throat he thought he could use her mouth like some naive slave-girl's cunt.

Sophie was too quick and too sly for him. She held him back, waiting until he was almost at the crisis-point, then squeezing his cock-tip and digging her thumbnails so hard into the glans that he screamed in pain. Seconds later she was ministering to his pleasure again, gently stroking, licking, biting until she had his whole body sweating and shaking underneath her. He was in heaven and he was in hell, so near to ecstasy and yet further away than he had ever been.

Just when she had him sobbing and panting, on the edge of orgasm, she withdrew, sliding her glossy lips along his shaft. He groaned.

'You've stopped. Why have you stopped?'

She slid up his body, kissed him with the taste of his own desire. Smiled down at him.

'Because I know what naughty boys *really* like.'

He growled, his hands exploring the curve of Sophie's arse beneath the absurd – but very stimulating – fur panties.

'Oh yes? And what might that be?'

'They like to lick a lady out.'

Emil gave a low, animal growling sound at the back of his throat.

'I can't wait to taste your pussy-juice. Just as soon as you've brought me off with those pretty lips.'

She shook her head and wagged a playful finger at him.

'I shan't. Not till you've satisfied me. Not till you've licked out my arse.'

A look of mingled horror and anticipation passed across Emil's face.

'No. You're crazy. Do *that*? What do you think I am, depraved?'

Sophie's smile grew broader, more lascivious.

'Of course. You just don't know it yet.'

Something had stolen all the strength from Emil Bernhardt's limbs. That was the only reason he could later think of for his total lack of resistance. One minute he was telling Sophie Ceretto no way, the next she was kneeling astride him, pulling down her white fur briefs, fragrant with her juices, pulling apart her buttocks and showing him the treasure within.

He didn't want to do it, of course he didn't. *What normal man would want to tongue out a woman's arse?* But it was such a beautiful arse that temptation whispered to him, *Try it, do it, do it now. You know she'll taste divine.*

And she did. That was the real wonder of it. He couldn't believe how good it felt, how good it tasted, to be inside her, to thrust in and out of her and feel her muscles clench at each thrust. To feel the pleasure bubbling and simmering within her until, with a long sigh, she allowed it to come to the boil and he felt the juice drip from her pussy onto his upturned face.

'Good boy,' she whispered. And bending over him, she kissed him; then slid down to take his dick inside her beautifully lubricated arse. How he screamed as she made him come, clenching her most intimate muscles about his shaft, squeezing the pleasure out of him in long, white spurts.

She lay across him, listening to the rhythm of his pounding heart; and to the whispered word which escaped, unbidden, from his lips.

'Mistress . . .'

A few hours later, Sophie drove away from Emil Bernhardt's house. She knew that wasn't at all what he had planned for her. Funny how things didn't always turn out the way you expected.

She stopped the car a safe distance from the house and took her handbag from under the seat. Opening it, she reached inside and breathed a sigh of relief.

She hadn't been wrong after all. There was a little something extra in there, exactly as she had hoped. A bulky envelope. So Stephanie had not failed her. She ripped it open and found a small packet, together with a letter. As she began to read it, a smile crept over her face.

A very cold smile.

Chapter 14

Emil Bernhardt was ravenous for sex. Not that he hadn't always been keen on it, but suddenly he couldn't get enough. No matter how much, no matter how adventurous or perverse.

And it was all the fault of that wilful slut Sophie Ceretto.

No, no. He mustn't think about her. Just letting her into his thoughts made his dick tingle and throb. It infuriated him to know he had desires that only she could satisfy. He had taken to screwing his women two at a time, three at a time, every which way; but still it wasn't enough.

Trixie was a good fuck, there was no doubt about that. She could do things with those breasts that could drive a man insane; smearing them with warm honey, wrapping them around his shaft and stroking him to orgasm after orgasm. But even Trixie's mammoth breasts and adventurous tongue were no match for half an hour with Sophie. Trixie and the other girls were too trusting, too unquestioning. He had made them that way.

Admittedly Stephanie Lace was different. She retained some of her wild rebelliousness, and any ride with her was sure to be exciting and unpredictable – but he couldn't help feeling that her wildness was little more than a reflex, not like Sophie's. Sophie's was tinged with a seductive hint of malice.

Emil relaxed on the bench seat in his private sauna and tried to imagine that the mouth closing around his balls belonged to Sophie instead of Stephanie Lace. The nails scoring deep furrows down his back were Trixie's. If he closed his eyes, Emil could just about imagine that they were Sophie Ceretto's too. He imagined them: a vampiress's talons, knife-sharp and painted crimson . . . or electric blue . . . or deathly black. That was the best thing of all about Sophie: every time you thought you had her all worked out, she reinvented herself. There was no question about it, talent like that mustn't go to waste. Sophie Ceretto was going to enjoy a very interesting position in his business empire – and he was going to enjoy it even more. She just didn't know it yet.

'Emil . . .'

The soft, sultry whisper teased its way into his brain. He could almost imagine that it was Sophie's voice and that she was standing naked before him – naked except for the slave collar which denoted that she was his and his alone.

'Emil, *darling* . . .'

His eyes blinked open, the lids heavy with condensation from the hot steam. He shook it away and his vision cleared.

'Sophie? *Sophie*? What are you doing here?'

She smiled at him, her lips shimmering blood-red through the curling steam. She was not naked, far from it.

236

But Emil was not in the least disappointed. Sophie was a wet dream in clinging black Lycra, metal-studded boots and leather gauntlets.

'Hello, Emil,' she breathed. His cock reared in joyful anticipation. 'Missed me?'

'You know I have.' Pushing Stephanie away, he reached out his arms. 'You've been gone too long, far too long.'

'Well, I'm back now, *darling*. And look, I've brought some friends with me.'

She stepped aside and three shadows surged up out of the semi-darkness. Emil stared from face to face, completely baffled.

'Inspector Gray... Sergeant Hope... *Chief Constable*? What...? I don't understand...'

Sophie laughed. This time the laughter was cruel, the smile exquisitely bone-chilling.

'You remember your friend the Chief Constable, Emil? Of course you do. He had such fun at your party. Well, he's come to pay you another visit, only this time he's going to arrest you.'

Emil felt hot and cold shivers running up and down his spine. Detaching Trixie's fingers from his shoulders, he stood up. He laughed nervously.

'Arrest me? What is this, Sophie, one of your weird jokes?'

'I'm afraid not,' replied the Chief Constable, motioning to the Sergeant to step forward. 'Put the cuffs on him, Hope.'

Emil struggled as the cuffs clicked shut about his wrists.

'You can't do this! I paid you off, all of you! The Vice Squad can't touch me . . .'

'Perhaps not,' conceded Inspector Gray. 'But we're not the Vice Squad. We're here to arrest you in connection with narcotics and kidnapping.'

Emil's jaw dropped. He stared at Sophie. She just kept on smiling.

'What . . .? How . . .?'

'Caution him, Sergeant,' snapped the Chief Constable. 'I think our Mr Bernhardt has a few things he'd like to tell us about.'

About a week later, Sophie went round to the Pink Pearl to see Laszlo. She found him sitting at one of the tables nearest the stage, watching Trixie go through her latest 'dance' routine.

He nodded a greeting as Sophie drew up a chair and sat down.

'Good to see you again, Sophie.' His grey eyes twinkled with amused lust. 'Come to ask for your old job back?'

Sophie laughed.

'You don't need me – you've got Trixie again.'

'Believe me, Sophie, I can *always* use talent like yours.'

She looked up at the stage. Trixie was three-quarters of the way through her striptease. A huge and raucous cheer went up as she unhooked the catch on her tiny sequinned bra and her immense breasts popped out. She beckoned two of the punters up on stage and giggled delightedly as they began rubbing warm oil into the vast expanse of firm, blue-veined flesh.

Laszlo shook his head and chuckled.

'The things that girl can do with a bottle of baby oil and a feather boa.'

'She's none the worse for what happened to her then?'

Laszlo shrugged.

'If she is, you'd never know it. She can't remember most of what Bernhardt did to her, and all she's talked about since she got back is whether Rick's going to give her star billing in the Christmas cabaret.' He stroked the back of Sophie's hand. She didn't draw it away. 'Thanks, Sophie.'

'What for?'

'For getting her back. Greta Garbo she ain't, but the Pink Pearl wouldn't be the same without Trixie. Or you,' he added meaningfully. Sophie chose not to notice the glint of passion in those grey eyes. 'How are you, anyway?'

'Oh... fine. A lot better since I found out what Bernhardt was up to all this time.'

Sophie accepted a champagne cocktail from a girl with pussycat ears and a long velvet tail. She sipped at it, then twiddled the swizzle stick reflectively.

'Tell me. I want all the details.'

She set down the glass.

'You know that Bernhardt was working for Paolo?'

Laszlo whistled.

'Is that so? I knew your ex-husband was slime, but surely things are still too hot for him to show his face over here.'

'Exactly. So Paolo's been keeping his head down and

using Bernhardt to do his dirty work. It seems they've been running a very lucrative string of brothels, using girls they've kidnapped and "trained" for the "hospitality" market. Some of the really popular girls have been sold as slaves to foreign millionaires. That's what was going to happen to Trixie and Stephanie if we hadn't got them out. Me too, perhaps – if Bernhardt had handed me over to Paolo.'

Laszlo nodded his understanding.

'So the drugs they used were powerful aphrodisiacs, designed to break down the girls' resistance and make training them easier?'

'Right. Anyhow, that was only part of the story. Paolo was using Bernhardt to get at me. He hates me, Laszlo, and he's angry. I got the better of him and he can't forgive me for that. He employed Bernhardt to get my trust, seduce me, put the frighteners on me and Andre . . . and turn me into a slave. Once he had me in his power, Paolo could humiliate me the way I humiliated him.'

'Only it didn't quite work out that way?'

'Fortunately not. Otherwise I'd be chained up in some harem in Algiers, not sitting here watching Trixie bring three blokes off with her tits.'

They laughed, but there was an uneasiness in their laughter. There was another question, still unanswered. It was Laszlo who voiced it.

'What about Andre? You think Emil Bernhardt killed him? Or Paolo?' He looked doubtful. 'You know, Sophie, Bernhardt may be several different kinds of shit, and he may well be into blackmail, but I'd never have taken him for a murderer.'

Sophie shook her head.

'He didn't kill Andre, I'm sure of that. Nor did Paolo. They don't have the strength of character.' She drained her champagne glass and rolled the stem between her fingers. 'You see, Laszlo, only a woman has that.'

The petite, dark-haired Frenchwoman was afraid. Afraid of being frigid again, and being unable to satisfy her philandering husband. And if that happened, he would leave her, she knew he would. And how could she go on living if Jean-Claude left her? Men were such bastards, all of them. They might seem to care in the beginning, but in the end they would all betray you. Even doctors.

Doctor Julian Simmonds ushered her into his consulting room and closed the door.

'Please, Madame Duclos. Take a seat.'

'Please, *Docteur*, you must call me Nanette.' She smiled a fragile smile, helpless and appealing. 'Can you help me, *Docteur*?'

'I'm sure I can.'

'Yes,' she breathed, crossing her slender legs to offer a glimpse of stockinged thigh. 'Oh yes, *Docteur*, I am certain that you are the only one who can help me, the only one I can trust.'

Simmonds sat back in his chair and folded his hands.

'Please, Nanette. Begin. You say that you and your husband have been experiencing sexual problems?'

'*Non, Docteur*, it is I, only I. It is not Jean-Claude's

fault that I am frigid. It is my fault that he is unsatisfied and looks for his pleasure with other women . . .'

She was deep into her story of cold sex and mistrust when the intercom buzzed. Doctor Simmonds sighed.

'What is it, Miss Graham?'

'You have a visitor, Doctor. A woman.'

'I'm busy, tell her to wait.'

'She says it's urgent, Doctor. Very urgent.'

'Very well.' Simmonds turned to Nanette. 'Please excuse me for one moment. I shall be back directly.'

She smiled up at him, radiantly trusting.

'*Oui, Docteur.* I shall wait for you.'

Alone in the consulting room, Nanette closed her eyes and let herself drift on the pleasurable warmth of her excitement. *This* was the one, she knew it. He was young, handsome, strong, dependable. She could tell him her sexual secrets, her urges, her fears, and he would not let her down. He would help her. She knew that it had happened before, that the other doctors had *seemed* to be the one, but that had been a mistake. In the beginning they had pretended to care, but sooner or later they had all betrayed her. That was why they had had to die.

A shadow fell across her face and she opened her eyes, expecting to see Doctor Simmonds standing over her, about to bend and plant a kiss on her lips. She knew he desired her, she had dressed especially for him . . .

But it was not Doctor Simmonds. It was Sophie Ceretto, magnificent and menacing in glossy black. The black widow. Heart pounding, Nanette made to spring up, but Sophie pinned her to the chair by her Versace shoulder pads.

'Where . . . where is *le docteur*?'

'Simmonds? I suggested he might like to go out for a while. I think it's probably safer for him that way, don't you Nanette? If he stayed, he might *accidentally* find some horse dope in his orange juice.'

Nanette tried to swallow but the lump in her throat was half choking her.

'I don't understand,' she said weakly. 'You're hurting me.'

The black-painted fingernails dug deeper into her shoulders.

'Jean-Claude owns a couple of racehorses, doesn't he, Nanette? Sometimes horses get sick. Sometimes they need medicine . . .'

'What of it?'

'You killed Andre, didn't you? It must have been so easy. He trusted you.'

'No! No, of course I didn't, I couldn't! You don't know what you're saying!'

'You killed Andre.'

'No!'

'Didn't you?'

'No, I told you! *Laisse-moi!*'

'Didn't you, didn't you, *didn't you?*'

Hands pressed over her ears, Nanette screamed out, 'Yes! Yes, are you satisfied now? Yes, yes, yes!'

Sophie was silent, waiting for an explanation. Sure enough it came flooding out.

'Andre had to die, don't you see? He betrayed me! He said I was special, but all the time he was screwing that bitch. I saw them together at the Dukinfields' party, on the yacht. My *Docteur* and that bitch Anastasia Madeley. I knew what they'd been doing. I saw his hand on her breast.' Nanette's dark eyes looked up into Sophie's face. They were filled with a kind of avenging madness. 'He had to die, he had to! I told him all my secrets and he betrayed me, just like all the rest . . .'

Sophie looked down at Nanette.

'You have caused me pain.' Her voice was a whisper of Siberian chill. 'No one causes me pain, Nanette.' She twisted a lock of dark hair about her gloved fingers. 'No one.'

'I don't receive pain from anyone. I give it.'

Postscript

Emil Bernhardt was far from happy about being locked up in a police station cell. On the other hand, there were consolations.

Like Police Constable Maryland, for example. Serena Maryland was young, pretty and rather sexy in her uniform black stockings. She also knew, far better than most, how to 'interview' a suspect in the most satisfying way.

Emil prided himself on his powers of persuasion, particularly where the female sex was concerned. PC Serena had withstood him for all of ten minutes before submitting to the power of his expert fingers and tongue.

Now she was repaying the compliment, kneeling between his legs as he sat on the edge of his bed; his cock sliding smoothly in and out of her round pink mouth.

He looked up as the cell door grated open, momentarily alarmed. But his expression relaxed and he pushed Serena's head down.

'Don't stop. It's nothing to worry about. It's a friend.'

Paolo Ceretto stepped into the cell.

'Well, well, Emil. Even in prison! Making yourself at

home?' He snapped his fingers. 'Tell the bitch to leave, this is private.'

The WPC got to her feet, wiping her mouth on the back of her hand, and scuttled out, closing the door behind her.

Emil's face relaxed into a smile.

'It's good to see you, Paolo. This place is beginning to . . . bore me. I was wondering how much longer it would be before you turned up to spring me.'

Paolo leaned his back against the wall and folded his arms.

'Actually, Emil, that isn't why I'm here.'

'Oh?' Emil's face fell. 'Why then?'

'You've let me down, Emil. Badly.'

'Yes I know, Paolo, but . . .'

Paolo shook his head.

'No excuses, Emil. You've let me down over our business deals and over that bitch Sophie, and frankly your incompetence leaves me no other option.'

'What do you mean?' Apprehension turned to alarm. 'How much longer before I get out of here?'

'You don't. You're going to plead guilty, keep your mouth shut and do your time. Understood?'

The blood drained from Emil's face. He began to shake.

'Paolo – you can't! You can't ask me to do this.'

'I'm not asking, Emil. I'm ordering. If you know what's good for you you'll keep quiet. And you won't mention my name – in fact you won't even *think* it, understand?' He drew his finger across his throat. 'Or else.'

Emil stared at him, dumbstruck.

'Paolo . . . I . . .'

'Fine, Emil, I think that's all perfectly clear. With good behaviour you should be out of prison in – oh – no more than five or six years. They're soft on criminals these days, no wonder this country's in such a mess. Maybe I'll buy you a drink when you get out. If you keep your nose clean.'

Paolo left in a swirl of cashmere and expensive after-shave, the cell door snapping shut with a sound like a whipcrack. And suddenly Emil Bernhardt was alone – more alone than he'd been in his entire life.

Saucy Suzy holds her own

NADIA ADAMANT

FONDLE ALL OVER

PLAYED FOR A SUCKER

Despite appearances – honey-coloured hair, doe
eyes and provocatively jutting breasts – East End
actress Suzy Fondle is not dumb. However, she is
a sucker for a handsome face and high-voltage
performance in the bedroom. Which, indirectly,
is how she ends up as a courier to a busload of
sex-mad singles on a backwoods tour of the
Continent.

Chaos threatens. Suzy has no knowledge of the
coach-tour trade and no foreign languages
beyond boudoir French. Ahead lies a trip rife
with underhand doings, foreign bodies of all
persuasions and a career as a scantily clad
performer in the naughtiest circus on the circuit.
It's funny, though, just how resourceful one
curvy girl with loose morals and a naughty mind
can be . . .

FICTION / EROTICA 0 7472 4038 8

JOHNNY ANGELO

GROUPIES

RED-HOT DAYS IN THE SUMMER OF SEX

SUMMER IN THE CITY

It's London in the summer of 1966 in the heady days of sex and drugs and rock and roll. And for the members of The Getaways, the country's hottest new group, the most important of these is sex!

There's Tony, the lead guitar, whose speciality is charming dolly birds out of their minidresses in the back of his E-Type. David, the bass player, is a sucker for the more sophisticated woman – like the manager's kinky wife. The rhythm guitarist, Sly, will pull anything for a laugh – and he doesn't care who's watching. Then there's Jud, the drummer, the innocent of the group. But now he's surrounded by fans with long legs, short skirts and wicked ideas, innocence is a vanishing commodity . . .

FICTION / EROTICA 0 7472 4091 4

A selection of Erotica from Headline

BLUE HEAVENS	Nick Bancroft	£4.99	☐
MAID	Dagmar Brand	£4.99	☐
EROS IN AUTUMN	Anonymous	£4.99	☐
EROTICON THRILLS	Anonymous	£4.99	☐
IN THE GROOVE	Lesley Asquith	£4.99	☐
THE CALL OF THE FLESH	Faye Rossignol	£4.99	☐
SWEET VIBRATIONS	Jeff Charles	£4.99	☐
UNDER THE WHIP	Nick Aymes	£4.99	☐
RETURN TO THE CASTING COUCH	Becky Bell	£4.99	☐
MAIDS IN HEAVEN	Samantha Austen	£4.99	☐
CLOSE UP	Felice Ash	£4.99	☐
TOUCH ME, FEEL ME	Rosanna Challis	£4.99	☐

All Headline books are available at your local bookshop or newsagent, or can be ordered direct from the publisher. Just tick the titles you want and fill in the form below. Prices and availability subject to change without notice.

Headline Book Publishing, Cash Sales Department, Bookpoint, 39 Milton Park, Abingdon, OXON, OX14 4TD, UK. If you have a credit card you may order by telephone – 01235 400400.

Please enclose a cheque or postal order made payable to Bookpoint Ltd to the value of the cover price and allow the following for postage and packing:

UK & BFPO: £1.00 for the first book, 50p for the second book and 30p for each additional book ordered up to a maximum charge of £3.00.

OVERSEAS & EIRE: £2.00 for the first book, £1.00 for the second book and 50p for each additional book.

Name ....

Address ....

....

....

If you would prefer to pay by credit card, please complete:
Please debit my Visa/Access/Diner's Card/American Express (delete as applicable) card no:

Signature .... Expiry Date ....